BARE YOUR BONES
THE AVERY HART TRILOGY
BOOK TWO

EMERALD O'BRIEN

Copyright © 2015 by Emerald O'Brien

Cover designed by Najla Qamber Designs
(www.najlaqamberdesigns.com)

Interior designed by Jade Eby
(www.jadeeby.com/services)

All rights reserved.

This book is a work of fiction. All names, characters, places, and incidents are either products of the author's imagination or are used fictitiously. Any resemblance to any events, locales, or persons, living or dead is entirely coincidental.

Printed in the United States of America.

*Mom, for your passion, encouragement, and strength.
And your sunshine.*

*Dad, for your wit, generosity, and support.
And your computer I've written all my stories on.*

*For the special bonds and memories with you both that
I'll always hold in my heart.*

And for the love we share. Always.

Chapter 1

CHARLA HELD HER HAND UP to the bloody print. The shape and size matched her own. She pressed it into the warm, sticky liquid, and pulled it away. Blood dripped from her fingertips and slid down her wrist. She pushed the door open with her clean hand. It made no sound as it swung open, and the porch light illuminated the hallway.

She knew what she was about to see, but she couldn't turn away.

Blood on the floor.

And the shoe.

And then the foot.

The path of light shone right up to their chests.

The blood on their chests.

She started to scream, and stumbled backward until she felt like she was falling.

She jolted awake and sat up straight in her seat.

The light burned her eyes, and she struggled to focus on the face of the soft voice she heard.

"Charla, it's alright, you're safe." She looked up and recognized January.

"I think I'm gunna be sick." Charla no sooner said the words, and January pulled her up, holding her steady until they reached the bathroom.

January gave her privacy and Charla tried to relax in her spot by the toilet.

A knock came from the door. "You okay in there?"

"Yeah." Charla called, and pushed herself off of the ground.

Lies and toilets had been her default since discovering the bodies of her family members in their kitchen.

When Inspector Cotter or January asked her how she was doing, she couldn't tell them the truth because she couldn't describe the feeling. A weird haze drifted through her head, and when it grew foggy, she couldn't even register the fact that her family was dead. The haze lifted when someone mentioned her parents, or her life as it was before, and in those moments she remembered that her family had been murdered. All of the pain would rush through her at once and made her physically sick. After each time she forced the pain from her body, she felt empty.

Charla rinsed her mouth with water and wiped it with toilet paper.

"Thanks." She told January when she emerged from the washroom. "Have you thought anymore about it?"

January pursed her smooth red lips, and pinned her blonde hair up in a bun. "You know I'd say yes, but it's not up to me."

"Inspector Cotter then?"

January gestured for Charla to sit down. "I haven't heard back yet, but if it's a yes..." Charla raised her brow and January nodded. "It'll be tomorrow."

"What's tomorrow?"

"We're picking Avery up from the hospital and taking you both to a secure location."

"So, maybe on the way?"

January nodded. "I think Cotter felt bad he couldn't be here with you until then."

He had been the only reason she was able to move on from what Patty revealed at the visitation, and actually be present for the burial of her family. Learning of the possibility that her aunt was really her mom. That she might have placed her with her real aunt and uncle, the people she had come to know as her parents.

And the insinuation that came with what Patty told her—that Arnold was her birth father.

Inspector Cotter was the rock that held her up, physically and emotionally. When he left after bringing her back to the station that afternoon, she missed his presence, and how it made her feel secure.

"I understand." Charla ran her fingers through her hair, and wrapped her sweater over her chest.

January had been more comforting, but no one could take the place of her parents, or her aunt, or whoever they were to her.

Finding the truth was the only thing that kept her mind from getting lost forever in the hazy fog that surrounded her in the quiet moments. In those moments reality seemed so far away.

"I'll put in a good word." January tapped her arm, and looked out the window to the hallway.

"This is the room I was in with my aunt --or mom..." Charla's voice trailed off as January looked back at her. "When she came back in to tell me the truth about Arnold."

"Hey, listen, whether we see Patty or not, you'll get the truth."

Charla rested her head back in her arms on the desk and tried to think of the questions she had for Patty.

The ones beyond who her real parents were.

The questions that got her answers to the whys.

The ones that helped her understand how she could have been lied to her whole life.

"Charla? There's one thing we are going to need you to promise."

Charla sat up.

"You have to promise that whatever the truth is, you cannot tell anyone. The dangers and risks that come with this knowledge are greater than you can even imagine."

Charla shook her head, and let her tears fall down her hot cheeks. January came to her side, held her for a moment, and swept her curly brown hair off her neck.

The cool air had a calming effect on Charla.

"I know it's hard, but it's for your safety."

"I promise." Charla wiped her tears away.

All she cared about was getting the truth for herself.

After that, there was no one left she'd want to tell it to.

Chapter 2

"How long is this drive?" Palfry tugged at his seat belt, and stared out the passenger's side window as they drove north.

Noah looked down at the clock. "Just under an hour, sir. By the time we arrive, we'll have a couple hours until dark."

"Right. After we're done there, we'll go straight to Officer Minicozzi."

Owen's bail hearing had been set for the next day, and Noah was sure he'd be granted the time to spend with his pregnant wife as he awaited trial. He was sure he would express his need to protect her, and the fact that they could still be in danger.

That Arnold Henderson could still hurt them.

It seemed like a logical move to Noah, but he couldn't get past the fact that his friend hadn't told him about the threatening phone calls from Bob Pope as soon as they happened.

"I understand you're friends with Officer Minicozzi, but after the visit, all communication between the two of you will stop for the duration of time this case is open."

Palfry was a gray-haired, overweight man, and Noah had yet to find a redeeming quality about him. Jacoby, the man whose cases he had taken when he retired, spoke of him highly. Noah remembered thinking that Palfry must be an intelligent man with power. Through one simple car ride, he learned that only one of those descriptions was correct.

"Understood, sir."

This was a fact he couldn't argue with. The Avery Hart case had been put into jeopardy on purpose— and accidentally— too many times to count while Ethan had been in charge.

"Let me make this clear, Cotter. Ethan has vouched for you. He told me you've got the most knowledge on the case. He says you're *the guy*." Palfry cleared his throat. "I'm honoring his wishes— for now."

Noah chewed on his tongue and tried to control his breathing. Palfry's breath stunk like stale coffee, and he was a close-talker, which meant attempts to avoid breathing while he spoke were futile.

"I'm confident that I can lead this case with the information from Ethan and yourself."

"I don't like it." Palfry shook his head. "You're too young. I don't understand why Ethan brought you in, but..."

The radio in Noah's car crackled, and an operator's voice came through over Palfry's.

"Units to 601 Mary Street."

"But I don't have to like it. I'm trying to do what's best for this case, Cotter, and if that's..."

"Sir." Noah held his hand up.

He recognized the address as Jennifer Hornby's and turned the volume up.

"... ambulance on the way."

Noah signaled and looked ahead for the next exit.

"What's this?" Palfry boomed. "What are you doing, Cotter?"

"That's Jennifer Hornby's residence."

"Hornby."

"One of Arnold Henderson's alibis. She came in for questioning, but she corroborated his story. Arnold killed her husband. She was the one having an affair..."

"With Arnold. I know, I read the files. I thought there were uniforms stationed there?"

"Surveillance, yes. They didn't report anything to me. Something's wrong."

Noah merged into the exit lane and Palfry flicked his siren on.

"Well, step on it."

Noah side-eyed Palfry and stepped on the gas. The secret location found at Tipper's Point would have to wait. Until then, Noah was thankful for the sirens that drowned out Palfry's voice and gave him time to think.

Chapter 3

"You've healed up nicely." Dr. Freebush nodded, and pulled Avery's hospital gown back down over her stomach. "Your head looks better already. I know you weren't happy when I delayed your release date, but we had to be sure there was no infection."

"Does that mean I can go?"

Dr. Freebush nodded and made a note on his clipboard. "Tomorrow morning, bright and early. I've prescribed antibiotics again, and you'll need to make sure you take them until they're finished this time."

Avery cringed when he said it, as if the fact that she was kidnapped the day she left the hospital was her fault.

He finished his notes and ripped off her prescriptions. "One more night, just to be sure, and then you're off."

"Thank you." He smiled and started for the door. "Dr. Freebush?"

He turned back. "Yes?"

"When will my stomach feel normal again?"

"Might be a few months. Just be patient."

He scurried out of the room and Sadie rushed back in right afterward.

Avery ached for his words to be true, but she knew it was impossible.

"How was your check up?"

Avery tilted her head down, and looked up at her. "You heard the whole thing."

Sadie shrugged and sat on the chair by her bed. Her smirk gave her away.

"I don't want you to go. I mean, I want you to be better, but I like getting to see you."

"Trust me," Avery picked up her cup and took a sip, "I wish you could come too, but it's for your own safety. You get that right?"

"What about you? I'll be worried sick."

"We can still text. Email too. I just can't tell you where I'll be yet. I don't even know."

"It's not the same."

"I know Sade." Avery held the cup against her lips.

"Josh and I will be here to see you off." Avery heard a whimper in her voice.

"Sadie, don't cry." Whenever Sadie showed any sign of weakness or sensitivity, Avery swore she felt sympathy pains.

She stuck her bottom lip out and shook her head. "You're gunna be okay, Avery."

"So are you." She managed a smile as Sadie leaned in for a hug.

It was gentle and short, but her smile grew as they parted. "Thanks for being here for me."

"I can't believe your parents didn't..."

"Sadie, you can stop saying that. I don't expect anything from them. I know better by now."

"I can't believe they tried to argue you'd be safer with them."

"I would have had to go home with them too, but I'm an adult, and I make my own decisions. Something they forget, just like they forgot about me when I went against their wishes. Honestly, even with all that, I'm not taking a chance on things ending up the way they have for Charla."

"You think Arnold could kill your parents too?"

Avery shrugged. "It'd be easy to find them. Easier than finding you and Josh. I don't think my parents get the fact that they could be in danger too. They think they control everything."

The thought of anything happening to her parents, regardless of their relationship at the time, was unbearable for Avery to imagine in any detail.

The thought had been enough to make her wince.

"I don't get it." Sadie studied her face before she reached down in her bag. "My mom sent you banana bread. I think she thinks you're her daughter too. You know that right?"

Avery smiled, knowing full well Sadie was trying to make up for the fact that her own parents had all but abandoned her. With banana bread.

"Give her a hug for me, okay?"

Sadie set the loaf on her bedside table. "I gotta go, but I'll be back in the morning. With Josh too; he has a surprise for you."

Avery looked at her with a straight face. "I'd rather not..."

"It's a good one. I promise." Sadie rubbed her arm and stood with her purse. "See you in the AM."

As she left, Avery watched her long skirt flow gracefully behind her, and heard her say goodbye to Ralph.

Ralph had assured Avery that Sadie would be safe, as long as they were apart. Arnold had no reason to know who she was to Avery, or what she meant to her for that matter, and Avery believed him.

"Hey Avery." He poked his head in the room. "I called Inspector Cotter and told him about your release. January's coming to pick you up tomorrow, alright?"

"Thanks Ralph."

He ducked his head out and waved at the same time.

She'd been hoping Noah would be her escort, but she knew he'd been busy looking for Arnold and watching over Charla at her family's funeral.

Avery was sure there were better ways of dealing with everything she was going through, but when she thought of Charla, she couldn't begin to imagine her pain.

Or Fiona's.

The girl she'd only known for a day.

She thought about her family and her lover Sam. Wondered if they had found a way to deal with the pain.

Fiona was gone— her suffering had ended— but Charla dealt with hers every moment.

Sometimes, in the middle of the night, Avery would cry herself to sleep.

The tears were for both of them.

Chapter 4

Noah parked in front of the house beside one ambulance and two police cars. He jumped out of the car and ran to the open front door.

"Body's in the bathroom." The paramedic nodded down the hallway. "She was dead when we got here. Officer's in there too."

Noah walked down the hallway and left behind the aggravating sounds of Palfry questioning the paramedic at the door. He took a few deep breaths, and braced himself for the same type of crime scene he found at Charla's parents less than a week ago.

As he approached, he saw a uniform inside.

"I'm Inspector Cotter. I'm in charge of the case."

"Pete Thompson." An officer stepped out of the bathroom and tugged on his pants. "I was out front when it happened. I was one of the officers assigned to this house."

He was a black man who looked young--younger than Noah, and his slender build barely filled out his clothes.

"You didn't see anything?" Noah started, but the officer held his hand up, and stepped to the side.

"This was a suicide."

He saw Jennifer's pale arm hanging out of the bathtub.

"Shit." Noah rubbed at his mouth and took a step in.

Jennifer Hornby looked like she was enjoying a bath.

Her eyes closed, her head rested on the back edge of the tub.

The water was murky— the bathroom pristine.

"No one came in and no one left. No struggle. Paramedic thinks she took too many pills." He gestured to the empty bottle in the garbage beside the toilet.

"You're sure no one's been in here?" Noah couldn't take his eyes off her light eye lashes that rested on her cheeks.

Pete nodded. "I'd have called you if there was, Inspector Cotter."

"Hey," Palfry stomped down the hallway, "your name?"

"Officer Pete Thompson, Sir. I was stationed here..."

"I know you were, so you want to tell me how you let this happen?"

Pete opened his mouth to speak, but Noah started first. "It was suicide, Sir. He didn't know."

The paramedic stood behind them and hovered over the conversation.

"I heard the 911 call go out, and I ran to the door but she had it locked. She wasn't answering, so I broke it down, and when I got in there, she was like that." He nodded to the body.

"What's this?" Noah asked and nodded to the mirror.

A white piece of paper hung from a small piece of tape.

"I think that's the suicide letter." Pete said. "I didn't touch it."

"Here." The paramedic handed Noah a pair of latex gloves. "Reporters just showed up."

Palfry sighed and Noah snapped them on before peeling the paper off the mirror.

"We need a full analysis of this body to rule out murder, regardless of the note." Palfry boomed.

The paramedic looked to the door and back at Palfry.

"Well, get on it! Where's the damn M.E.?" Palfry yelled and the paramedic nodded to his partner down the hall.

Palfry followed Noah to the living room, and carried on toward the front door, no doubt off to give a warm welcome to the Medical Examiner, Noah thought.

He turned his back to the big bay window to get the most natural light as he unfolded the paper.

I hope this letter finds Inspector Noah Cotter. He'll know what to do with it.

I write this letter in haste because I don't know when he'll come for me. When I heard about those girls, and what Arnold did to Maggie and the family, I knew I was next.

I thought it was Arnold who killed my husband from the very beginning. He wanted me for himself. When Grant didn't come home that morning, I had a sick feeling in my gut. I knew Arnold drowned Grant. I just didn't know the real reason why, but I think I do now.

I'm sorry I didn't tell you my suspicions right away, but the day you came to my house for my sister-in-law's phone number, Darrel Beelson was here. I told him what I suspected, and he told me to be careful. It wasn't a threat, but a warning, and I trusted him.

That's when I started to believe this was about more than our affair. The real threats came after. Arnold told me not to say a word or else I'd end up just like my husband. He didn't want me, romantically or otherwise, and that's when I knew Darrel was trying to protect me.

That's when I knew Arnold was a murderer.

I was selfish. I was looking after myself when I should have told you the truth, but you couldn't have protected me from him.

I've told you all I know. I wouldn't put it past Bob Pope to have been in on it all with Arnold, but Darrel is innocent, and I'm scared for him now. He did his best to look out for me.

This was the only way to tell my truth. The only way I could stop living in fear. I knew this was the right decision because I wasn't afraid anymore when I made my mind up.

Noah, be careful. He's not a very smart man, but he's strong, and dangerous. He's sick. I hope you catch him and he rots in jail or hell. Either way, it's not enough for what he did to those girls, to Maggie and her family, and to my poor husband who did nothing to deserve this.

Arnold-- if it is you that has somehow found this note before the police were able, I want you to know you didn't have any power over me in my last moments. I did not think of you, or our sexual affairs. I did not think of the threats you sent me and the fear you tried so hard to make me feel. I did not think about you at all.

I thought about meeting my husband again. The only man I've ever loved.

I died with no fear, Arnold.

You lose.

When Noah finished reading the letter for a second time, he realized Palfry was back in the room, holding his hand out for a better look. When he finished reading, he nodded.

"Let's get that in evidence." Palfry cleared his throat. "What do you think?"

"It confirms our suspicions regarding Jennifer Hornby. That Arnold did kill her husband and that she knew and didn't tell anyone because she was afraid. She was not working for Arnold. It confirms a lot."

"Beelson, you think he knows any more?"

Noah shrugged. "Hard to say, but we've got to get him in. He could be a target."

Palfry yanked at the tight waist of his pants. "Call it in and then we'll go to see Owen."

"What about Tipper's Point?"

Palfry shook his head. "It can wait."

He stomped out the front door, and left Noah alone, standing in the living room, the note in his hand.

He couldn't believe Jen Hornby took her own life, but the letter explained so much, and left him with so much guilt. She heard what happed to Fiona, and the Kent's and Maggie. She heard how he got to them even with police protection. Noah knew suicide was never the answer, and yet he could understand where she was coming from, and it all fell on his shoulders.

If he had insisted on bringing her in, or assured her she would be protected.

If he had come back to see her, or check on her, he might have been able to do something.

He might have been able to give her hope.

"Inspector Cotter?" Pete asked from the doorway. "I can take that to evidence when they come."

Noah handed the letter back. "Make sure I get a copy by the end of the day."

"I'm sorry I didn't get in here fast enough."

Noah shook his head. "You did everything you could."

Pete's shoulders rose and fell.

Noah saw the weight slip off of them and wished someone could have taken the burden from him.

"Cotter, let's go!" Palfry hollered from outside.

Noah grabbed his phone, dialed Ethan's number, and wished he was still the only one he had to report to.

Chapter 5

Avery waited in the dark hallway with Ralph by her side in the early hours of the morning.

"You know where we're going yet?" Avery asked.

"Yep."

"You're not going to tell me?"

"Nope." Ralph cracked a small smile.

Sadie came around the corner first with Josh close behind and a furry friend she recognized in his arms.

"Avery." Sadie whispered with a smile.

Avery nodded and instinctively covered her stomach with her hands. "What's Louie doing here?"

Josh set Louie on the ground and held his leash out to Avery. He was twice as big as the last time she had seen him just weeks before.

"He's for me?" Avery asked and looked from Sadie and Josh to Ralph.

"We didn't want you to get lonely without us." Sadie smiled and Avery noticed her eyes well up.

"I know he's just a little guy right now," Josh said with his arm still out, "but he'll protect you. You both need a friend."

Avery looked to Ralph who nodded, and she slipped the leash around her wrist.

"They already checked with me." Ralph sighed. "Ethan didn't think it was a good idea, but your friends were pretty persistent."

Avery smiled and lifted the pup into her arms. She felt the pull at her stomach, but no pain.

"Hi Louie, remember me?"

Louie sniffed her hair, and licked Avery's neck as he squirmed in her arms. She giggled, set him down on the ground again, and rubbed his head. When she stood up, Sadie was crying, and Josh's bottom lip was out.

"Thank you." Avery wrapped her arms around Josh and lowered her voice. "How did you know I'd want to keep him?"

"You distanced yourself from him from the moment I brought him to you. You didn't want to get close because you were scared you wouldn't be able to give him up. It's what you do with all the animals at the shelter. Give me some credit Avery. I know you better than you think." She let Josh go, and he winked at her.

Sadie held her arms open and Avery held her tight. Sadie sniffled before she whispered in her ear. "You're going to be okay."

Avery nodded and pulled away. Sadie wiped tears from her face and Avery rubbed her arm.

"It's just until they catch him."

Josh nodded and bent down to scratch Louie behind the ear. "He likes this."

Ralph's cell phone buzzed. "Time to go."

Avery looked at her friends and the feeling of forgetting something swept over her.

Was there something else she needed to tell them? Something they needed to know?

"Love you, Avery. Take care of her, Ralph." Sadie tried to smile when he nodded.

"You two are going to exit the way you came." Ralph nodded to them and turned in the other direction. "Let's go."

"See you, Avery." Josh nodded and Sadie waved as she turned around.

Avery followed Ralph down the long hallway toward the staircase with Louie's nails clicking against the tiled floor. Avery smiled down at him as he trotted away with them.

Ralph held the door open for her, and when she looked back, Sadie waved one final time.

Chapter 6

Noah rounded the corner and looked past Palfry to where Owen sat in his cell. His hung head rose when he heard them enter and he sat up straight as he made eye contact with Noah for the first time.

"Owen Minicozzi." Palfry pinched his pant legs at the thighs and pulled them up before he sat. "Never thought I'd see you in here."

Noah scratched at his five o'clock shadow and took a deep breath as Palfry brought out the recorder.

"We don't have to wait for my lawyer. I don't need one." Owen licked his lips and shook his head. "You both know my wife was taken by Arnold, and that he threatened to kill her if I did anything but what he asked. I'm not proud of the decision I've made and I recognize I failed the department, my colleagues, and my superiors."

Palfry shrugged. "The Boy Scout act might've worked on Ethan but it ain't gunna work on me."

"I'm— I'm just saying, all I've got is the truth."

Palfry chuckled and nodded to Noah.

"Start from the top." Noah quipped.

Owen nodded. "When I was given orders to go to Jen Hornby's to collect evidence that might nail Arnold Henderson to the murders, I went. I tried to find evidence, Ken can corroborate that, as I phoned him to look at phone records. Missy hadn't answered my calls all day and I was on edge. I thought maybe she'd gone to the hospital for the baby or..."

"Stay on track," Palfry said.

"I got back to my car, ready to head back," Owen acknowledged Noah, "and I found a cell phone on my seat. It rang right away and someone told me Arnold Henderson had my wife and if I wanted to see her alive again, I would take Fiona and Avery to him. He didn't say any more than that. Just that if I didn't answer my phone, Missy would be killed."

"Who called you?" Noah asked.

"At first I thought it was Arnold, but they spoke *of* him, so unless he speaks in third person, he doesn't fit the descript..."

"Just the facts, Minicozzi." Palfry barked.

"I was on my way to Fiona's, trying to decide what to do, when the cell rang again. Not ten minutes later. Same voice. Told me to take the girls to Tipper's Point. Told me where to stop and that more instructions would be given then."

"So you used your close relationship with the girls to take them." Noah said with a straight face, and out of his peripherals, he noticed Palfry smile.

"I didn't have time to think, Noah. My wife and our unborn child were all I could think about."

"But you thought of a plan to take Fiona and Avery. So you did think about other things." Noah looked to Palfry who nodded.

Palfry's enjoying this, Noah thought, and took a deep breath.

"You got 'em, didn't you?" Palfry boomed.

"I told Fiona we were going for a drive, and Avery that I was taking them to the station, and not to get Fiona upset."

Noah watched the grin on Palfry's face grow, but as the story continued, Noah wanted out.

"They figured it out on the way up. When I got to the drop off point, the voice called again, and told me to knock them out. He told me to drag them to a tree, tie them to it, and slip GPS devices in their pockets that I would find by the tree. I knew someone was there— watching me. They had the whole thing planned out." Owen looked to Noah. "I had to do it."

"So then— " Palfry glanced at his watch.

"I—I knocked them out." Owen closed his eyes, and Noah bit the inside of his lip, "I took them to the tree and I tied them. Not tight. As loose as I could. I slipped the devices in and I left."

"You were a good Boy Scout, right?" Palfry stood and looked down on him, "Did just what you were told."

"I didn't have a choice."

"Uh huh, tell it to the jury. Listen, we're here for the facts. For something that could help us catch Arnold. Did you ever speak to Arnold? Did you ever see him?"

Owen shook his head. "I drove as fast as I could to get to Missy. To make sure she was safe and then to call you."

"Yeah, thanks for the help." Noah shook his head and stood up with Palfry. "Real Boy Scout."

Owen's forehead wrinkled as he shot Noah a look.

Palfry chuckled. "That's right. That the end of the story, Minicozzi?"

Owen's eyes shifted from Noah and pierced through Palfry, but he continued. "I got a call telling me to dump the phone."

"Where?" Noah furrowed his brow. "You didn't tell me that."

"I tried to, but I couldn't see you until now. I dropped it off along the way to my place where Missy was, in a garbage can by the entrance to the park. Crown River Park."

"I'm getting a vehicle on it now." Palfry pointed at Noah, "Get his signed statement and meet me in the car. Don't let him feed you bullshit now, Cotter."

Noah smiled and nodded, but when Palfry was gone, they met each other at the bars.

Face to face for the first time since before the night he brought Avery and Fiona to the woods, and ultimately, to Fiona's death.

"I'm sorry Noah."

Noah shook his head and lowered his voice. "I've been over this in my head a hundred times. I get it okay, I get that you had to protect Missy, but why didn't you tell me?"

"I'd have broken his rules and he could have killed Missy. I wasn't trying to betray you, but I know I did."

"You broke my trust." Noah grabbed one of the bars. "I'm glad Missy is alright. That's the best I can do right now."

Noah slipped him the paper and a pen.

Owen nodded. "Can you come back later? I could try to help you..."

"No," Noah looked over his shoulder, "being an ass to you was the only way I could get you alone. Palfry's ordered me to not speak to you again until the case is closed. I get it, I get that you did what you have to do, but I can't contact you. I wanted to let you know."

Owen signed the form and the guard signed as a witness.

"You gunna forgive me?"

Palfry's heavy footsteps smacked against the tile, and when he rounded the corner, he waved to Noah. Noah looked at his old friend once more, before he followed Palfry on his way to the parking lot.

"There's been another murder."

"Arnold?"

Palfry shook his head. "Won't know until we get there, will we?"

When they got to the car, Noah took a deep breath of fresh air before he got in. "What do we know?"

"Vic's a young girl, left in Birch Falls Park. She's been cut."

"Like the others?" Noah asked.

Palfry shook his head. "Just one big slice from throat to belly."

Chapter 7

CHARLA LOOKED ON AS a tall man escorted Avery from the elevator into the parking garage.

"Stay here." January told her, as she hopped out from the driver's side.

Avery looked more pale than usual and Charla noticed a puppy jump out from behind her. It began to run ahead, and Avery pulled back on the leash, as January grabbed the bags from the man. Avery tucked her hair behind her ear, and revealed a small grin on her face, as she scooped the pup into her arms.

January threw the bags in the back and the man opened the door for her.

"Hi Charla, I'm Officer Ralph." he nodded and stepped aside. "Just call me Ralph."

When Avery looked up at Charla, her smile faded, but she nodded. "I'm sorry, Charla."

"Me too."

"Can you take Lou for a second?" She held him up and Charla scooped him into her arms.

She smiled down at the black puppy and stroked his head. "That's a cute name."

"Actually, it's Louie. My friend who gave him to me, he calls him Lou."

"Oh." Charla scratched behind the dog's ear. "Hey little Louie."

Ralph shut the van door behind Avery and hopped into the driver's side, while January got in beside him.

"Can you tell me now where we're going?" Avery asked.

"We're going to the safe house." Ralph said.

"One stop before that for us, though." January nodded back to Charla.

"Where?" Avery asked.

Charla looked ahead, and as January nodded, a grin spread across her mouth.

"We're going to find out who my real parents are. Or were."

Charla put the pup back in her lap and Avery shook her head. "I don't understand."

"Me either." Charla tried to collect her thoughts.

She kept her teary eyes glued to the window, although she had no idea where they were, because her thoughts drifted to memories. She tried to focus a few times, but the memories took over and so did her tears.

As Palfry and Noah ducked under the police tape, Noah spotted the body that laid on the path as the others had. As they neared, he noticed a large puddle of blood surrounding her.

"We got an I.D.?" Palfry asked an officer that stood nearby.

"Nothing on her, so not yet."

The medical examiner knelt over the body and another person took pictures.

"Just the one cut?" Palfry asked, and the M.E. nodded.

Palfry walked further from the police line, where a small crowd grew, and Noah guessed he was supposed to follow.

"Looks like Arnold."

"How could he take a chance out here, without anyone noticing?" Noah looked around.

"They're canvassing the area now. They'll ask the regulars who jog the path. The answer's clear though, Cotter. Nobody jogs this path after dark anymore. No witnesses."

Noah watched as a news van pulled up to the curb.

"Ethan had officers on duty here. I'll call them and..."

"Whoa, hold on. Ethan *had* men here, but I took them off."

"What?"

"It's not in the budget to have officers just sitting here around the clock."

"Sir, there is no place that security is more needed than here, and the Crown River Park."

"Crown River and Birch Falls parks are hundreds of acres combined. We don't have the man power, Cotter. I've still got them doing drive-bys. Frequent checks of course, but if they get another call, they respond."

"Why wasn't I notified of this?"

"Let me make one thing clear, Cotter," Palfry stopped and turned to him, "I'm not required to notify you about any of my decisions. It's the other way around. If Ethan had made better decisions while the case was fresh, I wouldn't have to babysit you and your team out here."

Noah would have left right then, before something happened that he'd regret, if the man didn't control the fate of his entire career. He couldn't think of anything to say that wouldn't get him fired, so he pressed his lips shut.

"You go ahead and check with those officers, Cotter, but if they saw anything last night, they would have reported back already."

"If we had them here permanently--"

"Are you questioning my decision after what I just said? I told you-- not in the budget. A budget being something you don't have to deal with, but it is my direct responsibility." Palfry noticed his voice was raised, and took a step toward Noah, "Anymore questions? No?"

Palfry stomped off, and when the officer he'd spoken with initially began to approach him with a question, Palfry jabbed his finger in Noah's direction. The officer came to Noah, and looked over his shoulder before he spoke.

"What crawled up his ass?"

Noah shook his head. "I'm the lead on this case. What have you got?"

"I think this is related directly to Arnold Henderson. Not as messy as some of the crime scenes have been, so it's him or a copycat. They're taking the vic to be examined, so before I go, I just wanted to point out that the vic was not shot."

Noah nodded, agreeing with his own theory, that the noise of a gunshot would have been too revealing. "Thank you. Anything else?"

"I just got word that a woman was reported missing last night by her boyfriend. Lisa Carson. Lives here with him in Birch Falls. No reports filed yet, but it could be our vic."

Noah thanked him for the updates and called Ethan. When he shared the news, he hadn't sounded surprised.

"It was just a matter of time."

"Yeah, we all knew that, but Palfry took the officers off watch here."

Ethan swore under his breath. "Listen, you remember what I told you. Don't cross Palfry. Just keep going on the trail, and keep filing me in."

"It's like he doesn't want Arnold caught."

"Oh, he does. His job depends on it. That's why he's acting like this. It's not personal, Cotter."

When they ended their call, Noah promised to have Ken send him the M.E.'s report on the dead girl, and updated security tapes from the area. He watched as they loaded the girl's body into the vehicle, and as he walked past the puddle of blood, he thought of Tamara Sweeten and Wendy O'Connor. He saw the crime scene photos, but seeing the dead girl in person made it easy to picture the other two lying on the path in a puddle of blood, or what was left of it after their trip to Tipper's Point.

The blood, he thought, had been almost drained from the others by the time they were returned back to the park where he initially shot them. This time, there were no bullet wounds, and more blood. If Arnold had killed the girl, he did it solely with his hunting knife, and finished it right where he started it— there in the park.

⁓

Patty welcomed them into her apartment and rushed to bring them each a cup of tea. The living room was tidy, dated, and smelled like old women's perfume.

Charla fiddled with her purse in her lap until Patty finished serving them.

"We appreciate your time, but we don't have very long. Charla has some questions for you." January sat back on the couch and held the tea cup in her hands.

"Yes, Charla dear, I'm so sorry for what happened at the visitation. I truly thought you knew, but I'm so thankful you've come around." Patty folded her hands in her lap. "Please, ask me anything you'd like."

Charla pursed her lips and took a deep breath. "Maybe you should just start from the beginning, where ever that is."

"Of course. Well, I'm a midwife, and I was still living in Toronto when --" she looked at January and back to Charla, whose tears were about to spill over.

"I'll just tell it like it is. A woman named Teresa Kent called me and said she would like to employ my services. She told me her sister, Maggie Prescott, was pregnant and wanted to have a home birth. I accepted the job, and lived with them for the last two months of the pregnancy. I grew close with Maggie and her sister and her husband, and when it was almost time for the baby to be born, Maggie came to me with her secret."

"She told me that she wanted to give the baby up for adoption, specifically that she wanted Teresa to keep the baby. I asked her why, and she wouldn't really tell me. I told her I wouldn't sign the paperwork if she wasn't honest with me. I just felt like something wasn't right. She told me she was not in a relationship with the father of her child anymore, and that she wasn't ready for a baby. Finally, she came clean. She told me she wanted me to forge the documents so it would appear as if her baby was really Teresa and John Kent's."

"So you did it?" January asked.

Patty shook her head. "She seemed almost fearful, but I couldn't tell if it was about having a baby, or what would happen if I didn't help them forge the documents. I told her when the baby came, she would want to keep it. I told her she needed to visit a proper doctor, which she had lied to me about, and that I could help her straighten things out. If I had known the father of the baby was a--" She looked up at Charla with tears in her eyes.

"How do you know who the father is?" January asked.

"Maggie confided in me that she had only slept with one person, and had gotten pregnant from that one time. I hear that more than you'd think. I believed her. Anyway, as time went on, I realized Teresa and John were unable to have children of their own. I think that's what changed my mind. Here was a woman who didn't want her child, and another who wished more than anything that she could have one. I told the three of them that I would do it. That I would sign the papers, send in the documents, and be their witness. This was of course, on one condition."

"What?" Charla heard herself whisper.

"That if Maggie had the baby and decided to keep her, that my papers would be ripped up."

"So she didn't want me?"

"No dear, the opposite. It happened just as I thought it would. Maggie had a baby girl and as soon as she looked into her big green eyes, just like her mother's," Patty nodded to Charla, "she decided to keep her. I could tell Teresa and John were disappointed, but it was Teresa who ripped up the forged documents. They seemed to support her. We went ahead and took you to the hospital, had you all checked out, and got you your birth certificate. All legal." Patty glanced at January, "Before I left though, Maggie named you."

"What did she name me?" She held her breath.

"Charla. Charla Prescott"

Charla sighed, wiped her tears from her cheeks with her sleeve, and Patty handed her a tissue. It was the answer she hadn't known she wanted to hear. Maggie was her mom and she named her.

"That year, I got a Christmas card from Maggie. In it was a picture of you. She thanked me and sent her best wishes. That happened every year, until a year ago." Patty got up and went to the kitchen. "I kept them all."

"I don't understand." Charla called.

Patty brought out the small shoe box and gave it to Charla.

"I didn't really either. All these years, I thought she kept you."

"My— my name on my birth certificate is Kent," She crumpled the tissue in her fist, "how is this possible?"

Patty pressed her lips together and shook her head. "She must have changed her mind."

Charla shook her head. "It doesn't make sense. She gave me up to be back with him?"

"Maybe she gave you to her sister because she never wanted anyone to know who the real father was?" Patty said. "Maybe she was afraid of him?"

"You've seen the news then." January cleared her throat. "I have the adoption documents for you to look over, Charla. I think it's time to go."

"So there are adoption papers? It was a legal adoption? How could I not know?"

"Closed adoption. They didn't intend for you to find out." January stood. "Thank you for your hospitality. I have to ask that you keep this information to yourself."

Patty nodded. "Oh, of course."

"But if she was afraid of him, why did she go back with him?" Charla stood and blocked the path to the door.

January took out her cell phone and held it tight. "I think she was a young single woman, who was afraid to have a child on her own. I don't know if Arnold abused her, or what happened, but they broke up for a period of time. I think maybe if she had known she would get back together with the father, she might have made a different decision. Maybe when Arnold became abusive, she was glad she made the choice she did."

"I don't...my mom never really wanted to be a mom." Charla shook her head. "Teresa I mean. She treated me like shit most of the time. Never really cared about me. Was jealous of my relationship with Maggie..."

"Your mom had pity on her sister not being able to have children. She wanted that for her. I know it was part of her decision." Patty walked over to Charla. "She must have been scared, Charla. Of being a single mom. Of Arnold. I don't know. I know she wanted you though. I know it like I know the sky is blue. She was trying to protect you in one way or the other."

January rested her hand on Charla's back, but she shrugged it off. Patty picked up the shoe box and handed it to Charla.

"She'd want you to have them."

Charla looked down at the box and turned back to her.

"Patty? Did you ever see either of them again?"

"No, I didn't. When I heard about her death though, and about your-- Arnold. I had to come pay my respects and see you."

Charla nodded. "Thank you."

"I wish there was more I could do, or tell you, but everything you need to know now is in that box." Patty put her hand in her arm. "She loved you. All three of them did."

BARE YOUR BONES

Charla let January guide her out with her hand on her back, and as they waited for the elevator, Charla wished she had more time with Patty.

As January received a text, she pointed to the stairs, and Charla followed her. She wondered if she had the adoption papers with her, or if they were already at wherever they were going.

January had the answers to her questions, and one answer in particular, she needed to know.

Chapter 8

NOAH GLANCED AT THE empty passenger's seat as the wind blew through his short hair.

No Palfry. No Problems.

On his last trip to Tipper's Point, he was following a hunch that turned out to be valid. After the officers and inspectors left the search, Noah had been alone at Tipper's Point, left wondering what the point of it all was.

Arnold had managed to get the girls to Tipper's Point with Owen's help, not to mention Bob Pope, his probable accomplice.

Noah wondered if Arnold meant to hunt Avery and Fiona down, shoot them, and slice them up the way he had his first two victims. Arnold's last encounter with Avery left her needing stitches, but she was alive.

Could he have spared her on purpose again, or did she slip through his fingers?

He turned onto Thorpe Road, and drove until he saw the broken down sign in the distance.

Arnold managed to escape somehow that night and Bob Pope took the fall. Noah shook his head, as the image of his bullet lodging itself in Bob's chest, and then Bob shooting himself in the head flashed through his mind. Although Arnold had eluded them all, the secondary location he took his prior victims to had been revealed. What the search crew found in the rundown trailer park had been in the back of Noah's mind for the past twenty-four hours.

Had Arnold had the chance, Noah wondered, would he have taken Avery and Fiona there like the others?

Noah pulled into the abandoned trailer park the way he came in that night, and he continued until he found the creek. He drove on the path alongside it, until the rust-stained trailer at the end of the path came into view. He slipped out of the car, and the gravel crunched under his feet as he approached the police car parked beside it.

"Pete?"

"Inspector Cotter." He reached out his hand and they shook. "I didn't think you'd show up."

"Sorry, things kept popping up. We the last ones in?"

Pete nodded. "All the evidence has been collected. You know, Palfry wanted the team to wait until he got here before they touched anything. You believe that?"

Noah sighed. "Doesn't surprise me."

"Then he never shows. We would have been waiting two whole days. Can you believe that guy? He should stick to pushing papers in his cozy office."

Noah shrugged and started for the trailer.

"No one's been out here for twelve hours. I came after leaving the Hornby's place, took over for another officer, and I've been waiting since."

"Okay, good." Noah opened the door and the metallic smell made him cringe. "You can wait out here if you like."

Pete nodded and held the door open to let the natural light in. "He didn't even bother cleaning up when he was done."

"He probably wanted the next one to come in and see this mess." Noah shook his head and studied the brown stained table in the middle of the room. "Any weapons found in here?"

"Just rope to tie 'em up. No guns. No knives."

The white tiled floor had sporadic brown spots around it, and the smell of urine wafted toward him when Pete opened the door wider. The windows were taped up and a wooden chair laid on its side in the corner.

"There was nothing else in here?"

"Nope. Pretty simple set up. He must have brought everything he used and taken it with him."

"Have you seen any kids around here?"

"No. Kinda strange. You'd think they'd come when they heard."

Noah stepped out of the trailer and stood in front of it. "The girls screamed. They must have. No one around to hear them."

"If anyone did, they didn't report it." Pete stood beside him and crossed his arms. "Why do you think he brought 'em up here?"

"Like I said, privacy."

"Yeah, but they were taken from Crown River and Birch Falls. Why shoot 'em there, bring them all the way up here to cut them up, and then take them all the way back and put them where he found them? Why not leave them here? No one would find them."

Noah shrugged. "Also meant no one had to go looking for them. Maybe he didn't want his secret place found. Maybe he just wanted them found. The way he left them."

"Sounds like a lot of trouble to me. Sounds like he was showing off. That he could shoot a girl, kill her, and return her to the crime scene. That takes balls. He could have been caught."

"He returned them at night, not many go running down those jogging paths after dark."

Pete shook his head. "Not anymore."

"Listen," Noah shoved his hand in his pocket, "there's been another murder."

He handed Pete his card.

"Where?"

"Birch Falls Park. I want you to keep an eye out there for me, alright? On your shift and off the record."

Pete took the card and looked back at Noah. "Wasn't there someone there?"

"Palfry took the guys off the schedule. He's just got drive bys now. If Arnold's going to be bold enough to go back there, or to Crown River, after everything that's happened— we're going to catch him."

Pete looked at the card and nodded. "Does that mean I'm on your case now?"

"Unofficially. Anybody gives you trouble, just tell them to talk to me, alright? Thanks for waiting for me. You're good to go, Pete." Noah started back to his car.

"Hey Cotter." Pete called to him. "You think he'd come back here?"

Noah stopped by his car. "We've had patrol here, waiting by the trailer this whole time right?"

"Yeah. Even shift changes were covered."

"Well then, if he's seen the detail here, he wouldn't. That's why I wanted security at the parks. He took the opportunity there, but there hasn't been one here. He wouldn't come in with you guys here. He's not that stupid."

"Right," Pete walked back to his car and called over his shoulder, "but the guy who shot himself probably was."

Noah followed Pete back out to the road, and thought about his last words.

BARE YOUR BONES

If Bob Pope had been working with Arnold, and never worked alone, would he be looking for another partner?

Chapter 9

THEY DROVE SOUTH, TOWARD the Greater Toronto Area, to the region of North York. Ralph exited off the main highway, and took a right at the next street.

"Is this where we're staying?" Avery whispered, so as not to wake Louie.

Ralph nodded. "I grew up here, actually."

"Is that why we came here?" Avery asked.

"No, I didn't make the call. There's a safe house set up here. It's on the outskirts, but it's busier than Crown River. More populated. It's changed a lot since I was a kid, but it's a good place for a safe house."

They drove past a few subdivisions, crossed another main street, and took a left onto a long road. Avery had lost count of the times she checked behind them to make sure no vehicles followed, never satisfied that they were alone.

BARE YOUR BONES

The road narrowed, and a police car was parked at the side of the road, covering a path that lead to a small park. It reminded Avery of a speed trap.

As they drove by, Ralph nodded to the big man inside. There appeared to be a dead end, but before that, a small house sat on the left. Ralph turned down the long driveway, and as they approached a pale blue house, Avery felt Louie's head pop up from her lap.

"Here we are." Ralph turned off the car radio and used his hand held. "Come in Blue, the hawk has landed."

Ralph turned back to her and winked.

A large man stepped out of the house and waited with his arms at his sides at the door. He looked like a club bouncer, or some sort of security with his bulky figure.

When they parked, the man strode over to the vehicle, and opened the back door.

"Please come with me." His deep voice boomed.

Ralph waved his hand, and the moment Avery slid out of the van, her stomach ached.

"You alright?" The man asked.

Avery nodded, and noticed him staring at Louie before he escorted them back to the door. Avery turned to see Ralph grab her bag out of the trunk, set it on the driveway, and fished a pack of cigarettes out of his pocket.

When she turned around, the big man held the door open for her.

The house smelled like lemons and Avery took a deep breath.

"I wasn't told about the dog." The man glanced down at Louie, before he closed the door, and took a black wand out of his pocket. "Lift your arms please."

Avery lifted them and he ran the wand an inch from her body, from top to bottom.

"Are you looking for a tracking device?" Avery looked up at him and he nodded.

He ran the wand over Louie, and the dog barked at him. The big man smiled for a split second, and it faded just as fast as he looked back at her.

"Have a seat." He nodded to the living room of the open concept home.

The living room was to the left, and the kitchen to the right.

"Can I take my dog out back? Or front?"

The man shook his head and reached his hand out for the leash. "I can."

Ralph came through the front door with the luggage, and dropped it where they stood, as the man took Louie toward the back of the house.

When he was out of sight, Ralph spoke. "He's a uh-- a man of few words."

"Yeah, I got that."

"Let's get settled in before the girls get here. You any good at cooking?"

Avery shrugged. "I mostly order out."

"Oh." Ralph's shoulders dropped, and he peeked out the front bay window. "Maybe January...or Charla, although I suppose she won't even be in the mood to eat."

"I won't either until I know what the deal is." Avery walked to the narrow hallway, and through the sliding glass door at the back of the house, where Louie sniffed the grass.

"We have this set up so you can live your life as close to normal as possible. It's... the new normal? Yeah."

Avery turned back to him.

"You'll still be able to teach your classes. No volunteering at the animal shelter though. You're too close to the people there, especially Josh, and Arnold could use that against you. No visiting your parents..."

"That won't be a problem." Avery muttered and heard a noise at the front door.

They turned toward it as January opened it wide.

"I want a DNA test." Charla spoke, and although she wasn't in sight, the words were firm and clear.

Avery heard Louie come back in the house. The big man handed her the leash again and grabbed his black wand.

Charla stopped at the door, and they all watched her as she stared at January.

"There's one being done as we speak, Charla." January nodded. "You'll know as soon as I do."

"Please lift your arms." The big man boomed.

"Who are you?" Charla spat.

"This is Blue." January stepped in the house and locked the door behind her. "Blue is with Avery."

"Blue?" Charla repeated and stared up at him.

He stared back at her until she lifted her arms.

"Where's my room?" Charla asked as he waved the wand around her. "I'm tired."

"I'll show you both to your room." Blue set the wand on the kitchen table and turned to the stairs.

"Room?" Charla and Avery exchanged looks.

The man started up the stairs and the girls followed. There were two rooms to the left and two on the right.

"Bathroom," Blue pointed to the far left and continued from there, "my bedroom, your bedroom, their bedroom."

They entered the room, and Avery was sure it wasn't more than one hundred square feet. There were two single beds against opposite walls, a closet by the door, and a window in the middle.

Avery noticed Charla clutching a shoe box in her arms. Blue waited for someone to say something, and when they were quiet, he left the room.

They heard his heavy feet clunk down the stairs and Avery set Louie down on a bed. He rolled over and over again, and Avery smiled until she felt Charla watching her.

"Could I get some privacy?" Charla asked.

"Yeah, sure." Avery picked Louie up and started for the door.

"Hey, it's nothing personal. I just need to be alone right now."

Avery wasn't sure how true the statement could be, so without turning around, she closed the door behind her.

⸺

January came upstairs and tried to get Charla to come down for dinner, but she declined, and stayed in bed. After January left, Charla sat with her legs crossed and set the shoebox in her lap. She took off the top carefully and set it to the side.

The first card had a picture of a Christmas tree, and she studied the picture before she opened it.

A black and white picture slid out. Charla recognized it right away as one of her own. A picture she had taken of a robin on a pine tree covered in snow.

The date in the bottom right corner was from two Christmases ago, and she could tell by the writing it wasn't her mom's— it was written by Maggie. Her mom never dated cards, but Maggie always did. She had a card just like this one.

Patty,

Merry Christmas and Happy New Year.

May it bring blessings of comfort and joy.

Charla's a photographer, so this year, instead of a picture of her, I'd like to send you a picture she took.

Talented and beautiful. Merry Christmas to you and yours, Patty. Love, Maggie

Charla set the card to the side, and grabbed the next.

Another card, a picture of her high school graduation portrait, and a message saying how proud she was of her little girl all grown up. Charla put it aside and opened the next.

Another short note and a school picture. She went through the next few faster than the first, tossing the cards aside, and hungrily reached for the next.

Dear Patty,

Merry Christmas

May your holidays hold a beauty all their own.

I hope you are well and the holidays have been good to you. Charla's getting all A's in school and she's growing up before my eyes. I want to thank you for what you did for me. You cannot know how much your words comfort me when I think back to our days together. You told me to be strong and I've tried to carry that with me, Patty. I've tried to pass that on to Charla. She may not always make the right decisions, but she comes to me with her problems and in truth, she's stronger than I am. Love, Maggie

It was her first year of high school, and she knew Maggie was referencing what happened with Avery. It was the only real mistake Charla made, and she had confided in Maggie.

She read through the next several cards. Nothing stood out, but the pictures created a time line of her

BARE YOUR BONES

life, and in each one, her happy smile had been built on lies.

She came to the last two cards, and read them each.

Dearest Patty,

Wishing you a very Merry Christmas

Thank you very much for your card last year. In addition to the picture of Charla I promised you, I also sent my new address. If you wish to send me cards, as I send to you, please use that from now on.

Isn't she beautiful? I look into her eyes and I remember the day I had her like it was yesterday. Sometimes, I worry about the future, but as long as I have Charla, everything will be fine. I know it. Thank you for everything you've done for me. Merry Christmas. Lots of love, Maggie (and Teresa and John say hello too!)

Charla looked at the picture of herself as a baby through her tears. She picked up the other piece of paper and saw her parent's address. It was her parent's home address Maggie had given them.

It must have been after she got back together with Arnold, she thought, and picked up the final card.

She must have been scared he would find it.

The last card had a picture of a much younger Patty and Maggie holding Charla. Their heads touched, and Patty had her arm wrapped around Maggie. They were both smiling down at Charla.

Dearest Patty,

Merry Christmas and Happy New Year

This is one of my favorite pictures and I made a copy for you. The best day of my life. I miss you, we all do, and are thinking of you this holiday season. You are probably helping another woman as she gets ready to give birth, and she's lucky to have you by her side. I look at this picture often and remember the times we were all together. I wish we could be together again this Christmas. My beautiful baby girl is already growing up. I have struggled with right and wrong, you know this better than anyone, but I hope my Charla never does. I hope when she is faced with a challenge, she takes the right path. Not the path of least resistance, but the one of courage. The one she knows is right. I thank you for the advice you gave to me when I was faced with the greatest challenge of my life. You chose the right path too. All the best to you and yours. Love always, Maggie (and Teresa and John)

That was it. The end of the pile.

You chose the right path too.

Patty told Maggie to keep me.

When the fact hit her, Charla burst into tears. She sobbed uncontrollably and pushed herself up from the bed. She opened a window and tried to breathe when she heard someone open the door.

She gasped before she saw Avery enter with Louie, and struggled to catch her breath again.

"Charla, I just came to check on..."

"Sh— she..."

Avery hurried over to her and rubbed her back. "Take your time."

"My— Maggie, she wanted me. I know it." A sound Charla didn't even recognize came out of her, and she gasped for air again.

"Of course..." Avery nodded. "Oh Charla..."

"She was protecting— me." Charla gasped for breath.

Louie tried to jump up on the bed, but when he couldn't, he licked at Charla's socks.

"He's trying to make you feel better." Avery picked Louie up, and set him on Charla's lap.

Charla pet him and took deep breaths. "They had an agreement. To protect me. I know they did."

"This has to be so terribly hard for you, Charla."

"My head hurts."

"Let me see if I can get you some Tylenol." Avery stood from the bed.

As the throbbing intensified, the lights went out.

"Avery," Charla hissed.

The hum from the power was gone, and the house became dark and silent.

Chapter 10

Noah spotted Darrel as soon as he walked in. He waved to Joe, and pointed to his regular booth in the back.

His and Owen's regular booth.

If it had been any other week in his career, Noah would have brought Darrel into the department, but he had worked over twenty four hours, and it was the only place he could force himself to go that wasn't home to bed.

He had to question Darrel again after Jennifer Hornby's death and suicide note. He had expected him to put up a fuss, and make Noah bring him in the hard way, but he agreed to meet within the hour. Noah was glad, because he couldn't fathom sitting next to Palfry again and remaining respectful until he had gotten some sleep.

"Back here."

Darrel stood from his chair and followed Noah to the back of the bar. They took a seat and while Noah took his coat off, Darrel kept his on.

"Is this the kind of interrogation where I can have a beer? Cause if not, I'm leavin'." Darrel said.

"It's the kind of interrogation that's off the record." Noah nodded to Joe, who grabbed two pint glasses. "I'm sorry about Jen."

Darrel shook his head. "I'm goin' outta my mind here. I can't sleep, haven't slept since Bob tried to blow his brains out, and now I can't eat. I'm not really livin' here. You gotta do something for me. Put me in witness protection? Something."

"Not how it works, Darrel." Noah waited until Joe brought their drinks and left again. "You have to give us something that can put him away."

Darrel reached for his glass but hesitated. "That's the only reason I'm here. Only reason I'm meeting with you. I might as well kill myself like Jen. You gotta help me. They are all gone."

"Okay, listen, I'll see what I can do. I'll see if we've got the resources to get you out of town. Is there a place you can stay until I contact you again? A safe place?"

"I don't know. Maybe." Darrel took a sip of beer, "Yeah, I'll find something."

"Think hard, cause I'm taking you there myself."

Darrel studied Noah and chugged his whole drink down.

Noah heard his cell phone buzz.

Ethan.

He slipped it back into his pocket.

"Darrel, if I'm going to help you, you have to give me something. Somewhere Arnold would stay. Why he and Bob were working together. *Something*."

"I gave you something--"

"Keep it down." Noah looked around them.

"I told you about Tipper's Point."

"I need something else." Noah said. "At this point, you know him better than anyone."

"You see what he does to living people who know him well?" Darrel held his hand up until Joe noticed, and nodded to him. "Look, Arnold and Bob were tight, just like Grant and I were. I thought I knew Bob..." Darrel grabbed Noah's glass and took a gulp. "They both liked to hunt, but so do I. I didn't see anything more there."

"So you wouldn't have thought Bob would murder anyone?"

"God, no."

"And Arnold?"

"In retrospect, yeah. Not Bob though. He was an asshole, sure. It's why his wife took the kids and left him. God, I can't stand to think of him in that hospital, half his face shot off."

"He did that to himself." Noah shook the image from his memory, "But Arnold was different?"

"Yeah." Darrel took another sip of beer and lowered his voice. "He--I think he enjoyed the hunt more than the kill. And he loved the kill. Christ, he loved to gut em'."

"Do you--" Noah started, but he waited for Darrel to finish chugging his beer. "Do you think they were working with anyone else?"

"You think I'd know that?" Darrel glared at him. "I want assurance that I'll be kept safe. I'm not saying anymore until you can give me that."

"I can't do that right now, but like I said..."

"Then I can't help you." Darrel wiped his mouth with his sleeve and stood. "If this is the part where you tell me not to skip town, save it. I'm getting as far away from here as I can."

"Darrel..."

He tripped over his own feet as he turned for the door. "Leave me alone. I told you before."

Noah stood and started toward him as he shuffled to the door.

"You promised." Darrel turned back and looked at him. His eyes were full of fear and sadness. "You promised you'd leave me alone."

"Darrel, let me take you somewhere safe."

"I don't know nothing. I ain't got nothing to give you." Darrel shook his head and pointed at him.

"You stay away from me."

He turned and left. Noah started to follow him, but stopped when he got to Joe.

"I'll put it on your tab." Joe waved, and Noah nodded before he left.

Chapter 11

AVERY HEARD HER HEART beating in her ears until the floor creaked outside their room.

Charla squeezed Avery's hand tight and Avery held Louie close.

"I'm coming in— "

January.

"Avery and Charla. Are you safe?"

"What happened?" Avery whispered.

"Stay calm and quiet." She whispered and the door closed.

The girls held hands, and thoughts of the mask loomed in Avery's mind.

"January," she whispered through her teeth, "what's going on?"

"When I say so, I want you to go to the window and open it. Do you understand?"

"Yes." Avery whispered.

"Charla?"

"Okay." Charla said as the lights flashed on, off, and on again. January stood behind the door with her gun aimed toward it.

"Clear!" Ralph yelled from down stairs.

"Clear." Blue called.

"Clear." January hollered as she slipped the gun back into her holster by her side.

"January?" Charla whimpered.

She opened the door. Blue entered, with Ralph close behind.

"This was a test." Blue said. "I had to see how fast response times were, and what you two would do in an emergency."

"Okay, Blue," Charla's voice was strained, "why couldn't you have told us it was a test?"

"I put together a plan and told January and Ralph. I wanted to check response times. I wanted to see your natural reactions. You followed instructions well." He looked to January and she nodded. "The police car you saw on the street coming in. That's my partner, Red. He was here in less than a minute. Ralph covered the front of the house until Red arrived, and I searched the home, while January attended to you two."

"You didn't panic and you did as you were told." January said. "That was important."

"Okay," Avery set Louie on the bed and stood. "If this is what you're going to do to us, how will we know if the next time is a test or if someone's come to kill us?"

"There won't be another test." Blue said.

"That's what you tell us." Avery crossed her arms.

"This isn't a game." His cold eyes stared at her. "I'm here to make sure you are protected. I take that seriously. I advise you to do the same."

Avery took a step toward him and lifted her shirt up until the bottom half of her bra was showing. The bandages were gone and ten knife slices had begun to scar.

"You want to tell me to take it seriously? How dare you. *This*," she looked down at her stomach and yanked the shirt back down again, "*this* was just a warning. I've been taking this seriously since I was fourteen. I've been preparing myself for this since then. I wasn't prepared enough. I got hurt. I watched people die."

Blue stared at her, and Avery assumed the others were too, but she kept her eyes on him.

Avery lowered her voice. "I have nothing against a test, or drill, but if you don't tell us first? I've got a problem with that. I lived this. We are living this now and it's all real. This is *not* a test."

"You've both been through a lot," January said, " and we want to make sure you don't have to do it again."

Avery sat down on the bed.

"If something like this happens again, or you feel something is wrong, you go to January." Blue spoke in the same tone as before, "You follow her instructions.

When the house is secure, we will let you know. Any questions?"

Avery and Charla looked at each other and Blue left the room.

"Take it easy guys," Ralph said, "sleep well."

January sat on the bed opposite theirs. "I know he comes off cold. He's being professional."

Neither of the girls spoke.

"Charla, the results are back."

Charla licked her lips. "Well?"

"Arnold Henderson and Maggie Henderson are your biological parents beyond question."

"Can I be alone now?" Charla asked.

January nodded. "If you need me, I'll be in the next room."

After she left, Avery got into her bed and snuggled with Louie.

Neither girl spoke and the air was heavy.

"Charla?" Avery whispered.

"Please," Charla sighed, "just leave me alone, okay?"

Avery slid under the covers with Louie and tucked him in. She grabbed her cell phone and saw three missed texts from Sadie.

Are you there yet? Wherever there is?

Everything okay?

We miss you.

As she answered them, another text alert made the phone vibrate in her hands.

Chapter 12

HE FOLLOWED DARREL TO a cheap motel on the outskirts of town, and watched him walk into the front office. He waited until Darrel got into his room before heading home.

He thought about watching out for Beelson himself, but he didn't have the time or energy. He believed him when he said he had no more information. That everything he knew, he had told them, and that he was scared. As Noah took a shower, he promised himself he would try to get Darrel some sort of protection until Arnold was caught. Maybe he needed to leave the country for his own safety.

Although he dreaded meeting with Palfry, and asking for a favor, he knew it was necessary. If anyone had the power to help Beelson— it was him.

When he got out of the shower, he found a text from January.

Security test was successful. Girls resentful. DNA results back. Positive.

Noah wasn't surprised after hearing how their meeting with Patty went from Ethan, but knowing the truth set even more factors into play.

They assumed Arnold was unaware of the fact that Charla was his daughter instead of niece. He came after her whole family, and although the team predicted he would or could do the same to Charla, it was also possible that she didn't mean enough to him to bother with.

Avery, on the other hand, was one of the last pieces of unfinished business for Arnold.

He made sure to do away with Fiona, and there was no way he would let another one go.

Girls resentful.

He wasn't surprised that Avery hadn't appreciated the security test, but he wouldn't have bet she'd spoken up about it. That was something Fiona would have done.

Avery has to know the severity of the situation. She has to know security is top priority.

He slipped under his cool sheets and checked his cell phone once more before leaving it on the night stand. He tried to sleep, but not knowing the specifics of the safe house, and how they were doing— how Avery was doing— bothered him.

He needed sleep, he told himself, and he knew of just one way he would be able to rest.

He grabbed his cell phone and typed.

Avery, it's Noah. How are you doing in there?

He hit send and groaned when he noticed the time.

Two. She's probably asleep.

He set the phone back on the nightstand and pulled the blanket up over his head.

His phone dinged and he grabbed it.

Avery.

As well as can be expected. How's it going out there?

Still looking. Doing our best.

He set the phone back on the night stand, as if creating distance between them would stop him from speaking to her. Stop him from becoming more personally invested in the case.

He stared the cell phone down, and when it dinged, he grabbed it.

Will you be coming here?

No. Can't. You're safe though. They'll look after you.

He realized talking to Avery wasn't making him relax. It made him want to be there with her.

I wish you were here.

Noah shook his head and grinned. Their thoughts were the same, but she had the guts to actually say it.

One wrong word and he would cross the line.

Use this number in case of an emergency. He hesitated, and then typed *I'm here for you.*

It was the best he could do. The best he could give her under the circumstances. He wanted to be there to protect her.

No one needed it more.

Arnold always came back for his victims, and they were convinced Avery wouldn't be an exception.

Good luck, Noah. I'm counting on you.

The words lit a fire inside him. He wanted to tell her he was doing everything he could. That he would do everything in his power to catch him, but when Arnold fled before the police arrived, his window of opportunity had closed.

He wanted to tell her he would catch him for her.

Good night Avery.

He knew he had to find another window. When the next chance came, he had to make sure they were more than a step ahead. Arnold was a salesman, a hunter, and a husband. These were the things he knew well. Noah had underestimated his intelligence, but there were inconsistencies in his personality.

In his actions.

He was smart enough to get away with transporting his victims to a separate location and back again without getting caught, but not organized enough to make sure one couldn't get away from him. Not organized enough to clean his secondary location in the trailer at Tipper's Point.

Arnold is not a clean or organized man.

He was smart enough to use Owen to transport the girls to him. Smart enough to use GPS trackers. Smart enough to run before the police came when the girls had outsmarted him. He left his dirty work for his partner to finish at Tipper's Point that night.

He left his partner, Pope, as a loose end.

Or had they agreed for Bob to end his life before he could be caught?

Arnold was strong and bold. He knew that much to be true, but he put the inconsistencies of his actions down to Bob Pope, and wished he would wake from his coma to be interrogated.

He was thankful that Avery hadn't seen Pope put the gun to his head and pull the trigger.

Or the pieces of his face explode through the air.

She had turned at just the right time to think Noah had shot him again.

Noah wondered if that could be the reason they hadn't found Arnold yet.

Had they turned their head at an important moment and assumed something they thought they knew?

Find the missing pieces to the story.

Noah kept the cell phone in his hand, and despite the finality of his last message, he hoped she would text him again as he began to drift off.

Chapter 13

CHARLA WOKE IN A SWEAT. The room was gray and she could tell it was close to sunrise. She couldn't remember the nightmare exactly, but just before she woke, she was standing in the middle of her street. It was the night she came home to find her family dead, and when she stumbled to the street, she saw Arnold. He stood in the middle of the road more than twenty feet away, and it was only for a split second before she woke, but she knew it was him.

She struggled to catch her breath, but knowing reality was worse than her dream, she began to hyperventilate.

If Arnold had still been there that night, she thought, and heard something move beside her.

Avery sat down on the bed, next to her knees, tucked up to her chest. Charla looked up at her, and Avery propped her pillow up.

When Charla sat up straight, she was able to catch her breath, and she rested her head back against the pillow as she wiped the sweat from her forehead.

"I have them too. Nightmares— " Avery whispered.

Charla nodded. "It's real life too. Our worst nightmares are really happening."

She looked at Avery, who nodded, before re-situating herself to face Charla.

"I'm finding it hard right now to just— even to get my thoughts together." Charla whispered and waited for Avery to speak. When she didn't she went on. "My aunt, really my best friend in life, was my mom, Avery. Even trying to get past this, or through this, or even on top of this is impossible right now, because nothing trumps the fact that my dad is a killer."

Charla shook her head at the realization. She said it and it was true.

"I can't even imagine how you're feeling Charla. I think I'd be confused and stunned. I didn't want to talk to you about it until you were ready though, because I can't even pretend to put myself in your shoes. I don't want to pretend to know how you feel, or tell you it's going to be alright, but I can tell you one thing. You're in charge, Charla. If you want things to be okay, you're the only one who can help yourself."

"I don't even know where to begin." Charla's voice choked out.

"You have to take it a day at a time. Little by little. You've got the truth now. You can decide what to do with it and what it does to you. It can make you stronger."

"Arnold has--is-- killing all these people. Innocent people. He killed everyone I love and he might want to kill me, but you know-- I don't even really care about that part." Charla pushed the tears away from her eyes and curled up on her side. "I can't even get to that part, where we are now, because there's no one left. I have no one to go home to Avery. He killed the only people who truly loved me."

Avery rubbed her back and the feeling soothed her as she sobbed into her hands.

"It's weird to talk to you about my family, when it's linked to you like this. I saw how hurt you were in the hospital. I didn't see those scars..." her gaze fluttered from Avery's stomach back up to her face, "but I saw the hurt, so you don't have to apologize. The cuts, were they deep?"

"Not very," Avery ran her fingers over her stomach, "we think they represent the years it's been. Since what happened when we were fourteen. You couldn't have known— "

"I wish I hadn't told Maggie." Charla shook her head. "I should have pretended it never happened."

"You felt guilty. It was natural to tell her." Avery stood up and grabbed her pack from beside the bed. "I'm being honest. I don't blame you at all for this. It was a mistake. We've both made them."

Charla nodded and watched her leave the room to change.

She wasn't sure if it was guilt leaving her body, or talking about her family, but she felt better than she had since the night she found them. She felt drained, tired, and weak, but she also felt hope for the first time.

Hope that she could build a true foundation for her life for the first time.

Chapter 14

ON THE WAY TO ROOM C, Noah saw Palfry further down the hallway with another officer, and hoped to slide by without being seen.

"Ah, Cotter." Palfry called down the hall and waved him over. "This officer just came from the Sweet Grass Motel and a body was found that relates..."

The words hit him hard.

"Beelson. What happened?"

"How did you know?" Palfry shooed the officer away with a nod.

Too little, too late. The feeling sunk in his gut and marinated there along with the rest of his self-doubt.

Noah filled him in on the previous night.

"So he had no new information to tell you?"

Noah shook his head and took a deep breath. "What happened to him?"

"Slashed and gashed, Cotter. When were you going to tell me you spoke to him?"

Don't start this with me. Not now.

"This morning. I was going to ask for protection for him."

"Yeah, well, he would've been no use to us. You told him to stay at a motel. Don't let a guilty conscience cloud this investigation."

Do you even know what a conscience is?

"I got the medical examiner's report back on our dead vic from Birch Falls Park," Noah wanted to interrupt, and ask him why the report came to him, but decided it wasn't a battle worth picking, "Lisa Carson, twenty-five. Looks like it was Arnold. I had the report sent to your office. I want you to meet with her boyfriend. He says he doesn't know why she would have gone to Birch Falls Park. She's not a jogger, and as far as he knew, she never went there before."

"Yes, sir." Before he could move an inch, Palfry's breath wafted toward him.

"Where are you off to now?"

"Meeting with," Noah stopped himself from saying team, knowing Ethan's involved was supposed to be limited while he was in the hospital, "Ken, our tech analyst. Looking for updates and new info."

"Right. He's been given the security footage from The Sweet Grass for review."

"Is there a T.O.D. on Beelson?

"Not yet. Must have been between the time you left him and five this morning. Motel called it in when they got a complaint from another guest in the room next door. Get me something good, Cotter. By the end of the day."

"Yes, sir." Noah waited while Palfry studied him.

"What are you waiting for?"

Noah brushed past Palfry toward Room C.

Had it been right after I left, he thought, or had Darrel been sleeping?

He knew Arnold was coming, just like Jen Hornby, and they should have been protected.

When he entered, Ken had three laptop screens in front of him, and was engrossed in the footage projected onto a larger screen on the wall. Noah slammed the door shut behind him and Ken jumped.

"Sorry Ken. I just ran into Palfry."

Ken rolled his eyes and nodded. "Dick."

Noah smirked and walked around the table to view the footage. "This is from the Sweet Grass Motel?"

"Yup. Here." Ken pressed a few buttons, and Noah glanced at the dry erase board while he waited.

No one had written anything new since Ethan's last words more than a week before.

Tipper's Point.

"Here." Ken looked up at the projection. "Arnold goes into the motel through the back exit. And," He pressed another button, "Here he is on camera two, in the hallway, just outside Beelson's door."

"How did he know? He knew which one was his without going to the front?" Noah leaned on Ken's chair and watched.

"Never went to the front. Must have watched him check in. There. He breaks the knob. Storms in. One minute later, he's out. Leaves out the back, and gets into his black truck, but here," Ken paused the video, and zoomed in on the license plate. "It's blurry, but this is a fake. Doesn't match his real plates, but we know he's driving in the same truck."

"Okay, hold on, let's get the team on conference call." Noah dialed the number from the speaker on the table.

"He must have followed him." Ken shrugged. "Right? I mean, like you said, how else would he…"

"Ralph and I are here, Noah." January's smooth voice came on the line.

"What's going on?" Ethan's voice cracked in.

"How ya doin' boss?" Ken asked.

"Fine, enough with the small talk, what's the deal?"

Noah told them about the previous night with Beelson and described what Ken had showed him on the screen.

"He must have been following him. He must have followed him to the pub where I asked him to meet me." Noah sat down beside Ken.

"Noah, this is beside the point," Ethan cleared his throat, "but it's worth mentioning that you should have told me about meeting with Beelson. Keep me informed, alright?"

"I will, Ethan. I planned on telling you. Hell—I even planned on telling Palfry."

"He's still using the same truck," Ken said, "and I think it's safe to say he's not getting rid of it. Just changing the plates."

"He's killed them all. His whole group of friends." January said and the sound of plates clanging together filled the air.

"It also means he didn't follow us to the safe house." Ralph said. "Sorry for the noise, just getting breakfast."

"All well there?" Ethan asked.

"Blue and Red have the whole thing together. They've thought of everything." Ralph said. "Taking Avery to work soon."

"Good." Ethan said.

"So Beelson was scared?" January asked, "But he had nothing new to report?"

"No," Noah said, "but when I went out to Tipper's Point yesterday, officer Pete Thompson was out there. He also responded to the Hornby residence. He got me thinking. Arnold used Owen, but as far as we know, he could have done the same to Bob Pope. I think Bob was his partner. It makes sense because I feel like there are two profiles to this murder."

"Keep going." Ethan said.

"Some of it seems organized and thought out. Some of it though, seems messy, literally. He left the trailer blood stained after cutting up the women. It was probably in rough condition before, but he didn't spend any time trying to hide it. Now we've got another vic, Lisa Carson, and everything points to Arnold, but it's different too. Location and type is the same, but she wasn't shot, or taken to another location. She also wasn't..." Noah searched for the words, "he only cut her once, unlike Tamara and Wendy. It could be someone else, unrelated to Arnold, or..."

"He's working with someone else." Ethan said. "Okay, so let's work with the theory Pope was his willing accomplice. Who did what?"

"Well, I think Arnold was the braun, and Pope was the brain. What if he's got another partner now and they killed Lisa Carson together?" Noah asked.

"You think he found someone else to work with?" January asked. "He doesn't need anyone else to help him kill. He proved that with Beelson."

"If he's used to working with a partner, maybe he *made* someone else help him?" Ethan said. "Like he did with Owen."

"Might have had a hunting buddy no one knew about." Ralph said.

More clanging noises filled the background.

"I'll ask Charla if there's anyone she thinks he was close with." January said. "Ralph, enough with the plates."

"Yeah," Ethan coughed, "maybe it was just Arnold, and he didn't shoot the girl because he thought the noise would attract too much attention in the park. Maybe he thought there was security there."

"You alright boss?" Ken asked.

"Yeah. I'm stuck in the hospital in a damn sling and now I'm sick. Chest infection. Imagine that." Ethan's personality was back. "Where could I have possibly gotten that from?"

"One other thing." Noah said. "Palfry says Lisa's boyfriend doesn't understand why she would have been at Birch Falls Park. Apparently she never went there."

"Right, well check that out," Ethan coughed again, "Beyond that, I think we have to focus on his next target."

"Avery." January whispered.

"All units know who we are looking for and what he is driving. The fact that they haven't come across him yet bothers me." Noah tapped Ken on the shoulder. "Ken's going to check road surveillance to see where the truck goes and track it as far as we can."

Ken nodded and started to type.

"Palfry thinks things aren't moving fast enough." Ethan said.

"I've been running from place to place, doing everything in my power to catch him," Noah said and started to pace the room behind Ken, "but if he's going to take security off the parks..."

"Listen, give Palfry the info Ken's got, and hopefully that'll stave him off for a while."

"He's unbelievable." Noah huffed.

"Suck it up." Ethan said. "I gotta go. Quick. What's your next step?"

"Review the footage. Meet with Lisa's boyfriend and see if I can't find a connection between Arnold and the vic."

"Right. Talk soon."

The speaker clicked.

"Call with any developments." January said.

"Will do." Noah hit the end call button.

"Palfry needs to get laid. That'd turn his frown upside down." Ken chuckled and popped a disc into the computer. "Now that I think of it, January too."

"What's that?"

"A copy of the tapes I just showed you, for you to give to Palfry. Like Ethan said, get him off your back for a while."

"Thanks. That was fast."

"Yeah, well, I get more work done around here without January distracting me, if you know what I mean." He winked at Noah and laughed. "I wish Ethan were back though, no offense to you, but this place isn't the same."

Noah shook his head, and took the disc when it popped out of the laptop.

"I'll be right back. Will you work on following Arnold's trail for me? Get that on disc too?"

"Already on it."

"Good. I'll be out following that trail as soon as you're finished. Until then, text me Lisa Carson's address." Noah walked around the table to the door and turned back around. "Ken? If you were Arnold Henderson, where would you be?"

Ken's chest heaved, and he looked at the dry erase board.

"I'd want to stay under the radar, but…" He stared at the map.

"But where would that be?"

"Somewhere I could still hunt—animals or girls."

Chapter 15

Avery was mesmerized by the fog rolling into the backyard while January played with Louie in the living room.

"He's such a sweetheart." January tickled his stomach.

Her cell phone vibrated, and a message from Sadie popped up on the screen.

How is everything going?

Avery typed back, *Okay, going to class soon.*

Good luck. Let me know how it goes.

January looked out the bay window. "Blue's back with groceries. Ready for work, Avery?"

"Ready when you are." Ralph put down his paper.

Louie ran to the front door, and Avery ran after him.

Blue unlocked the door, and Avery scooped him up before he ran out.

"All clear?" Blue asked and Ralph nodded and he placed two bags of groceries on the counter.

"Have you heard anything from Inspector Cotter?" Avery asked.

"We spoke earlier today when you were both in bed. No developments." Ralph tapped the newspaper on the table. "Arnold's not in here, but he's in all the ones back home."

Blue whistled. Avery released Louie and he ran behind the counter to Blue. He came running back out with a black rubber ball in his mouth.

Avery smiled at Blue, but he didn't seem to notice, and kept his eye on Louie.

Louie raced around the kitchen, and when he came back to Avery, he dropped the ball in her lap.

"Sorry Lou, I can't play now, I've got to go." Avery took the ball and rolled it across the floor to the kitchen.

January's cell phone rang and she walked into the next room before answering. Ralph stood from his chair and grabbed his jacket from the couch.

"Think I could take Louie for a walk later?" Avery asked.

"Ralph? Come here for a minute?" January called from the other room.

Ralph was out of the kitchen before Louie had time to notice he was on the move and ran after him. Blue smiled at Louie and Avery averted her eyes. She had a feeling he didn't want to be seen smiling.

"We're going to be late." Avery whispered as she picked up her shoulder bag.

She checked her cell phone, but there were no new messages from Sadie or Josh.

Or the person she wanted to hear from most.

Chapter 16

"Inspector Cotter." A young man opened the door to the apartment.

"Kevin Newburn. I'm-- was Lisa's boyfriend." Noah noticed a woman at the kitchen table. "That's Lisa's mom, Vivi. Come in."

Vivi looked over to Noah from her sunken dark eyes, and slipped a cigarette between her lips. "What happened to my daughter?"

The cigarette bobbed up and down and she lit it while she studied Noah. He wondered if she was thinking about how young he was.

No one said anything about his age, but he always felt he was being judged on it. That it exposed his level of experience.

"We're trying to find out ma'am." Noah followed Kevin to the kitchen table. "Could I ask you both some questions?"

"Of course. I told the officer I spoke to, the one who was there when we..." Kevin cleared his throat. "Identified her. I told him Lisa didn't go to that park. I don't know why she was there."

Vivi stared, deadpan, past Noah, out the apartment window.

"Can you tell me what happened the day she went missing?"

"She and Vivi had lunch and then we had dinner together. She told me she was going to see a movie with her friend Michelle. They were going to have a girl's night. Michelle said she never showed up. The building, Jaunt, is only a ten minute walk from here. She walked because we don't have a car. I shouldn't have let her walk alone."

"So between here and Jaunt, that's when she went missing." Noah asked.

"Right." Kevin nodded and looked to Vivi. "She seemed normal."

Noah turned to Vivi. "Did anything out of the ordinary happen that day with Lisa, or was there anything unusual going on?"

She started to shake her head, and her eyes welled up before she took another puff.

"Is there anything else either of you can tell me?" Noah asked. "Anything you feel is relevant to Lisa's murder?"

"No." Kevin shook his head. "I don't-- does this have anything to do with Arnold Henderson?"

"We're not sure." Noah said.

It was the truth.

"I just wish I had walked with her." Kevin looked down at his hands on the table. "I'm sorry Vivi."

Vivi rested her hand on Kevin's.

"My Lisa," Vivi said, and looked straight at Noah, "she didn't like to walk alone. She'd call me, or stay on the phone with someone 'til she got where she was going. She didn't call me."

"Me either." Kevin shook his head.

"Was she afraid in this neighborhood?" Noah asked.

"No, it's a good neighborhood." Kevin said.

"She told me a while ago, maybe a month or two," Vivi looked to Kevin, "that she felt like someone was following her. Maybe that's why?"

Kevin's forehead wrinkled. "She never told me that. She said that?"

"Did she mean one specific person, or just people who were behind her on the sidewalk in general?"

"I don't know." Vivi looked to Kevin, "I told her she was being silly. If she thought someone specific was following her, she would have told me who, wouldn't she?"

"I think she would have told me."

"Okay, well is there anyone you feel would want to hurt Lisa? Stalk her? A past boyfriend?"

"She had some weird ones." Vivi looked at him, and although her blank stare couldn't tell him what drugs she was on, he was sure he could have guessed.

"She would have told me if she felt like she was in danger."

"Any ex's she saw recently?"

"No," an ash from her cigarette fell onto the table, and Kevin wiped it into his cupped hand, "shit, sorry."

Kevin nodded. "I don't think anyone was after her. I heard about those girls. The ones Arnold Henderson killed."

"We're not ruling it out--" Noah started, but his cell phone rang. "One moment, sorry."

He stood from the table and walked to the door. "Cotter."

"It's Bob Pope." Palfry panted. "He's awake."

Palfry stood with a doctor outside Bob Pope's room, and as Noah approached, he waved him over.

"His children and ex-wife are in there now." The doctor said.

"What's happening?" Noah asked, "He just woke up?"

The doctor looked from Palfry to Noah. "I notified the department that he was being taken off life support at the request of his family. That he would likely pass away. I called as soon as he opened his eyes and tried to speak."

Palfry nodded to the room. "We need to talk to him now."

"He's stable for now, but his vitals are weak. I'll need to be in the room..."

Palfry nodded and pushed the door open.

Noah stood stunned for a moment, and anger flashed over him when he realized no one had contacted him about Pope's status.

But Palfry knew.

"Doctor?" Noah asked.

"Bailey." he said and hung back.

"Doctor Bailey, who did you notify that he was being taken off life support?"

The doctor looked at Palfry.

"Well come on." Palfry grunted.

Noah pushed his anger aside when he saw Pope's family standing beside him. Half of his head was bandaged and he looked drowsy, barely able to keep his eye open.

He held his daughters hand.

"We need the family out." Palfry said, and as an afterthought, "please."

His daughter squeezed his hand and whispered something to him.

Something close to a smile creased his lips.

The woman and two teenagers shuffled out of the room.

"Bob Pope--" Palfry started.

"Bob, I'm Inspector Noah Cotter. Do you remember me from the bar that night? Jerry D's?"

Noah paid no attention to Palfry, and sat down beside Pope, who nodded.

"Bob, you have to tell me what happened. Are you working with Arnold Henderson?"

Bob nodded and opened his mouth to speak, but closed it again.

"Take your time. I need to know everything."

Bob licked his lips and before he spoke, he drew in a shuttered breath.

"He blackmailed me."

"What?" Palfry said.

"He told me," Bob licked his lips again, and the doctor brought him a cup of water, "he needed me for an alibi."

Noah nodded. "For what?"

The doctor tipped the cup to Bob's mouth and he drank. Dribbles of water ran down his chin.

"He confessed to me that he killed those girls. Told me it was just like hunting. When I..." he looked up at Noah, "when I met with you, I suspected, but I didn't know. I swear. He didn't tell me 'til after that other girl was killed. Wendy something."

"Keep going." Noah looked at the doctor, who gave him more water.

"I said no." Bob swallowed and stared off across the room. "He told me he'd hurt my kids if I didn't."

"If you didn't what?" Noah asked.

"If I didn't keep his secret. If I didn't help him." Bob looked at the doctor. "My head."

The doctor was about to speak, but Palfry waved him off.

"Bob, what happened? What did he make you do?"

"I had to take the officer's wife. Tie her up. I had to bring the rope and tracking devices to Tipper's Point. To the location he gave me. For the officer."

"Good, keep going Bob." Noah said.

"I didn't want to kill her." Tears fell from his eye. "He told me if I didn't get them both, my kids were as good as dead. He can do that."

"I know." Noah said.

"I failed."

"Is that why you shot yourself in the head, Bob?"

Bob swallowed hard. "I didn't want him to use my kids anymore. He was gunna pin it all on me. I failed him and he was going to kill them to get back at me. I thought--"

"You thought what?" Palfry boomed.

Noah wanted to tell him to leave, but he remember Ethan's words, and bit at his tongue.

"Mmmuh," Bob moaned.

"You've both got to leave, now." Bailey checked a monitor beside Bob.

"Thank you, Bob." Noah nodded and started to leave.

"We're not finished here." Palfry said.

"Oh yes you are." Bailey pointed to the door. "This is my patient. Get out."

"Come on." Noah said, and Palfry shook his head, but followed.

"Can you believe that shit?" Palfry asked as he stormed down the hallway.

"I think it's the truth. I think Arnold used him."

"He could have told us where Arnold is hiding." Palfry pressed the elevator button several times and waited.

"All due respect sir, but he couldn't even talk anymore."

Palfry stared him down, but the elevator door opened, and broke his focus. They got in and when the doors shut, the tension was palpable.

"I went to see Lisa Carson's boyfriend."

"And?"

"No leads so far, but I have to talk with them again."

"The video you left me, does it tell us where Arnold is?"

"No, just where he was and what direction he went in."

"Follow it and then report back." The doors opened, and as Palfry stormed out, the elevator shook.

Noah wanted to ask why no one reported to him when the call came in about Pope being taken off life support. He wanted to shout at him and tell him he had no business being in the field or even inserting himself in the case, but he knew Palfry kept the news from him for a reason.

To try to sink him.

On the way to the parking lot, he dialed Ethan's number, and filled him in.

"Would you call January and Ralph to tell them?"

"Yeah, sure," Ethan said, "listen. Don't let Palfry throw you off track. Take control of this thing, Noah."

"I'm trying."

"I know. Where are you headed?"

"I'm going to see if there are any camp sites or motels east of Crown River, within an hour. Arnold's truck went that way last night after he killed Beelson."

"Alright, listen; it might be time to go on the offense."

"How?"

"I say we use his own game against him. Bait him and trap him. We know he's close, and we know he followed Beelson, so we make him think the girls are in a certain location. We lure him there and then we trap him."

"I don't--"

"Don't say anything now. Just think about it, Cotter. We are running out of options. The girls wouldn't be in danger. We'd use decoys or something. Just think about it while you're searching for him alright? Think about how much easier if could be if you got him to come to you instead. Let me know."

Ethan hung up and left Noah wondering if the plan was even something Palfry would go for.

If he did, and they could get Arnold's attention, it might work.

If they used the right bait.

Chapter 17

IF AVERY'S STUDENTS HAD been her age, Blue would have stuck out like a sore thumb at the back corner of the room. Instead, the man sitting beside him appeared to be older than he was.

"I apologize for missing our last class," she saw a woman in the front row lower her head when Avery looked her way.

They know.

Avery cleared her throat. "And I'd like to try to make up for it and fit in the next lesson plan today as well."

A young girl, Jade? She thought her name was Jade, stared up at her with wide eyes.

"Your assignment last week was to take a photo of an object that society deems ugly and make it look beautiful. Make it look like something people would take interest in, instead of grimace away from. You had an extra week to turn it in—"

The man beside Blue held his hand up.

"Yes?" Avery tried to smile.

"I was wondering if you would be reimbursing us for the cost of the last class you missed?"

"Pardon?" She swallowed hard, and squinted to see him.

"You missed the class, and didn't even give us any notice." The man looked around, and another woman in front of him nodded her head. "I don't have time to stay longer today, and I took this course thinking it would be finished before the fall, so I don't know when or how you planned on making up for it—"

"I am sorry, sir. I understand if you can't stay longer today, but throughout the regularly scheduled time, I assure you we will cover all the course material." Avery crossed her arms and walked behind her desk. "If you'll all turn in your assignments, we can start—"

A knock on the door captured everyone's attention, and Blue stood as the door opened.

Ralph poked his head in. "Ms. Hart, can I see you for a moment?"

Blue strode to the door, and the man beside him stood.

"Yeah, he's got the right idea," he stepped beside the woman who agreed with him, "I'm done with this class."

"I'm—" Avery shook her head, and watched the woman follow him.

"Sweetie," she stopped in front of her, "maybe with a few more years, you'll gain some more experience teaching, and you'll learn the importance of punctuality and responsibility."

Avery's mouth opened, but no words came out.

The woman shook her head and followed the man out of the room. Blue held the door open for her and nodded his head toward the hall.

"One moment, please." Avery's face was hot.

She licked her lips as she walked to the door. She saw her former students leave through the back door, and when she turned the other way, she saw Noah standing by a row of lockers. Ralph stood beside him and Blue remained in front of the door.

"Avery, I wanted to talk to you for a minute." He looked at Blue, and back at her, "Is everything okay?"

Avery tucked her hair behind her ear, and looked at Blue.

"Guys, I'm just taking her down the hall here, alright?" Noah asked, and Ralph nodded.

Noah put his hand on her back and guided her a few feet away.

"What's wrong?" He whispered.

"It's just my students. A couple just walked out."

"Quit?"

"Yeah, I guess I'm just overwhelmed. What's going on?"

He stared at her and his warm eyes searched hers. "There was another murder. A young woman about your age."

"Where?"

"Birch Falls Park."

Avery felt silly for even worrying about her class as the words hit her. She stared off past him, wondering how she could let that bother her with the reality she was dealing with.

Why did I come back here? Why did I think I could go about my life, like everything was normal...

"Avery," She looked back at him, and he stared deep into her eyes, "I'm not telling you this to scare you. I need to know if you knew Lisa Carson?"

Avery shook her head. "No, I don't think so. Is that the girl?"

"Yeah, she lived in Birch Falls with her boyfriend, Kevin Newburn. Do you know that name?"

She shook her head again.

"Avery," his gruff voice softened, "I'm worried about you. Maybe you shouldn't have come back to teaching so soon?"

"Maybe not."

"Are you nervous? Do you feel—"

"No, it's not even that. My students paid money to be in my class, and if I can't be reliable, I shouldn't be teaching them."

"Listen, don't put so much pressure on yourself." She nodded, and tucked her hair behind her ear, "I know it's been difficult, but don't think because you choose not to teach, you're somehow weak, alright?"

"I just wanted something to take my mind off what's going on. Something to make me feel like this doesn't define me. That he doesn't control me," she looked up at him as he took a step closer, "by fear."

"He doesn't control you, Avery." He whispered. "You decide what's right for you, okay? Not because you think it sounds like the right thing, but because it feels like the right thing."

She nodded and looked past him to where Ralph stared. Blue looked up and down the hall, and checked his watch.

"I have to get back in there. Will you be at the house sometime soon?"

"I can't. I have to keep looking for him." Noah turned down the hall, and held a hand up to Ralph. "If you need to talk, you can text me, okay?"

Her heart beat faster, as she remembered their texts from the night before, and nodded.

He looked down at her, and she saw something in his eyes.

When neither spoke, Avery started back to the room, and he followed.

"Thanks, Noah."

"Anytime."

Blue held the door open for her. "You've still got a few in there."

She smiled up at Blue, and walked back in.

"Ms. Hart," Jade called as she entered the room, "we want you to know we don't feel the same way they do. We know what's been happening, and we hope you don't let a couple of insensitive asses ruin this class for you, or for us."

All eyes were on her.

"Thank you." Avery took a deep breath and smiled at her.

Jade's eyes lit up. "Does that mean?"

"I'm not letting anyone ruin this class for *us*." Avery said, and heard the door close behind Blue as he walked back to his seat. "Where was I?"

Chapter 18

Avery opened the door to their room, and Louie bounded in as Charla set the file down on her bed.

"How was your class?" Charla asked.

Louie jumped up on Charla's lap and licked her cheek.

"Rough start," Avery set her shoulder bag down, "but I'm glad I went."

"Charla?" January called, and stopped at their door. "Charla, I'd like to ask you some questions if that's alright?"

"I guess."

Avery sat on her bed, Louie followed her, and January sat down beside Charla.

Charla waited.

"Did Maggie and Arnold ever go away on vacation together?"

"A few times. I don't really remember where though. I think they went down south somewhere for their honeymoon."

Charla vaguely remembered the pictures from their trip hung in their home.

"Did any of your family ever own a cottage or anything like that up north?"

"No, we don't have anything like that."

January nodded. "Okay. Were you over at their place a lot?"

"Yeah. I never knew he abused her though."

"No, I believe you. Did they ever have company over? Friends, while you were there?"

"Not really. Not besides my parents. I didn't go over as much after high school, so I wouldn't know after that."

"You don't remember anyone ever being there when you were?"

"Yeah, but I don't remember their names. I didn't see them enough to remember, and Maggie never spoke about any of them. I think they were more friends with Arnold."

"Did you have any suspicions about his affair?"

Charla shook her head. She felt her cheeks burn up and she fiddled with her hands in her lap.

"What did you know about him?" January asked. "Who was he to *you*?"

Charla thought for a while and spoke when the silence was too much to bare.

"He was funny. He always made me laugh. He made everyone laugh. Especially my dad..." She looked down at her hands, as they shook in front of her.

"Take a deep breath, it's alright." January said.

"He couldn't cook and he didn't clean, but he did all the yard work. He loved to be outside. He loved to hunt."

The words hung in the air before Avery pushed off the bed and rushed out of the room.

"I didn't mean to..."

Louie ran after her.

January shook her head. "It's okay. She'll be alright. Continue."

"He liked to play cards, Euchre, with my mom and dad. He's strong, physically, and he loved to travel for work. He was an eye ware sales rep."

January nodded. "Who was he to you though, Charla?"

"He was nice. Nice enough. I've always been closer to Maggie. I guess because she's a girl? He came to my graduation. I don't know, he was nice to me. You're asking me about a man I thought was my funny Uncle Arnie. Now I know he's a killer, and it makes me sick to think of him as that, never mind my own dad!"

"Did you think he loved you?" January pressed on.

"I thought so." Tears slipped down her hot cheeks.

"Do you still think he loves you?"

Charla shook her head and looked down at her fingers. "I don't think he's capable of love. Not after hearing what he's done. Is he a sociopath? Is he sick or did he change sometime, when no one was looking?"

January sat with her for a moment, before she got up. "Did you have any questions about the file?"

"It's pretty straight forward." Charla sniffed and wiped her tears, "Teresa and John adopted me before I was even a year old."

"Did you have any questions?" January's voice was smooth and low.

"Yeah," Charla handed January the file back, "but I can't ask them now, can I?"

She shook with anger as January took the file.

"I'm sorry Charla, but we need to know what you know if we can hope to think like him. To catch him. I'm sorry I had to ask."

A chill spread over Charla's skin as she sat alone in the quiet and wondered what her biological father was doing.

Who he was hurting.

Who else he was planning to hurt.

Chapter 19

"I THINK IT'S TIME we put that plan of yours in motion, Ethan." Noah sat across from Ken and rested his arms on the table.

"Good." Ethan's voice came from the speaker.

Ken raised an eye brow and peered out from behind his computer screen.

"Care to fill us in?" January's words were drawn.

"We are going to trap him." Noah said. "We are going to set a trap for Arnold, and anyone else who might be working with or for him."

"We have to make him think he knows where Avery and Charla are." Ethan said, "We have to make it so he thinks he can get to them. That's how we get to *him*."

"How?" January asked. "You don't plan on using the girls, do you?"

"No." Ethan said. "Decoys. They might be the only people left alive we know he wants. Avery at least."

"I don't know if that's a good idea." January said. "I've been operating under the impression that Arnold already knows where they are, even though there doesn't seem to be a way he could have followed us without us knowing. Is this a waste of time?"

"There's a first time for everything, I guess." Ken shrugged, "I agree with January. I feel like we should focus on finding his vehicle."

"Who knows if he'll buy it," she asked, "and what if it doesn't work, and he lashes out, or leaves?"

"Listen guys," Noah stood from his seat, "I've been trying to track him down and no one has seen him. He hasn't been in any hotels, motels, camping grounds. Nothing. He's murdered Darrel Beelson, we know that from the video footage. And Lisa Carson, who seems to have no connections to anyone involved with the case."

"What did the boyfriend say?" Ethan asked.

"Boyfriend and mom of the victim were there. They said she was supposed to see a movie with her girlfriend, but she didn't show. They didn't think anything unusual was going on beforehand, although it was suggested to Lisa's mom that she felt like someone was following her. She didn't tell her boyfriend though. Thing is, she was walking to the movies to meet her friend. He could have picked her up randomly, but Arnold always gets them from a park. Why would he pick a random woman up off the street to bring back to the park?"

"Maybe there aren't any women in the park anymore?" January said.

"Could have been Arnold was stalking her." Ralph said. "Maybe she could feel it. Women have that instinct, you know?"

"Did you talk to her friend? The one she was supposed to meet?" January asked.

"No."

"Talk to her friend. Girls usually tell their girlfriends more than anyone. If she was seeing someone else, if she had an issue with an ex..."

"Okay, I will," Noah said, " but the point is, we're out of options. I'm going to be watching the Crown River park myself tonight thanks to Palfry. Arnold's making bold moves right under our noses, but we can't get to him. We've got to try something different."

"I think we need to find a safe house, and have Noah go back and forth from it. It needs to be in a deserted area, so we can see who is coming and going. Look for old abandoned buildings, but something you could live in." Ethan said. "We need him to think they are there, and maybe he'll be on the attack. Maybe he's watching you, Cotter? Maybe he's waiting on you to make a move."

"Do you think Palfry'll go for this?" Ken asked.

"He's got to. This is Cotter's operation." Ethan said. "I'll convince him. This has to work, but Cotter, don't go near the real safe house. Got it?"

"Got it. So we're doing this."

"When?" January asked.

"We'll need time to lay it all out. We need to get a young blond officer. She's got to look like Avery from a distance. We'll have her near the windows of the place. Noah has to come and go from the decoy house at night. Maybe we'll be ready at the end of the week?" Ethan coughed. "Maybe more. Depends on how fast Arnold picks up on it."

"So we are doing it?" Ken asked.

"Yes." Noah stood over the desk. "I'll start making arrangements. Ken, you find the location. I'll find a double for Avery. We start tonight. I want to go there tomorrow night."

"We can't be too hasty. It might be too soon." Ethan cleared his throat.

"This is our chance."

"Anything we can do?" January asked.

Noah thought for a moment. "Yeah, there is."

Chapter 20

Charla didn't lift her gaze from the dark cloudy sky when Avery came back into the room.

"You're feeling sorry for yourself."

She shot Avery a look.

"I know you are because I was too. I play a pretty good victim, but you're rivaling me right now."

"What are you talking about?"

"Sure, we're forced to be here, and we've both been forced into our situations, but I don't blame you. If everything is what we think it is, I got myself into this. I went to the news to tell them about my potential involvement. I told them I was attacked by the same mask. I told them so they might have a lead. I'm the one that got it wrong. I'm the one that got Arnold's attention. I'm just as much to blame as you, but I don't blame you and I don't blame myself anymore. This whole thing goes beyond us Charla. That's why I'm not upset with you."

Charla looked up at Avery with tears in her eyes. "Why are you telling me this?"

"Because Arnold is doing this on his own. Arnold is killing people. He would be a killer regardless of what you and I have done. It's all fresh and it still hurts. That's why I walked out of the room when you were telling January about Arnold, but I should have stayed. I think I know what January was trying to do."

"No," Charla fiddled with her necklace, "you did't need to hear that."

"I do."

"Why?"

"Because if we're going to do everything in our power to make sure he's caught, and that we're not his next victims, then we have to know the enemy. January was right to ask you those questions. He was a man behind a mask to me. He really is a monster, but I won't be..." she bit her lip and sat down across from Charla, "I won't be as scared if he comes back if I know who he really is."

"I don't even know that Avery."

"You might know more than you think."

Chapter 21

"Kevin told me you'd be calling." A soft and feminine voice on the other end sighed. "How can I help?"

Noah leaned back in his chair and chewed on the lid of his pen.

"Kevin says Lisa was supposed to meet you at the movies. Is this true?"

"Yes. We were supposed to meet at eight so we could get good seats, but eight came and went and so did the movie start time. I texted her and got no response. Then I called her when the movie started. Nothing."

"What did you do next?"

"I called Kevin. Asked if she was there. Thought maybe she forgot. I drove the way Lisa would have walked, and I didn't see anything. We called the police and searched the area."

"What did you think had happened?"

"I don't know. Something bad."

"Why?"

"Lisa would never just leave. I knew something was wrong."

"Was Lisa seeing someone else? Someone Kevin and her mom didn't know about?"

"Like cheating? No. No way."

"Do you think Kevin would be capable of hurting her?"

"No, no. He didn't do it. He loved her."

"Was there anyone who would want to hurt her?"

"No, not that I know of. If Kevin and Vivi couldn't name someone..."

"Lisa mentioned to her mom that she didn't like to walk anywhere alone. Both her mom and Kevin knew this. Did you?"

"No, she never told me that. I mean, it doesn't surprise me. I wouldn't want to walk alone at night either. I should have offered to pick her up."

"Do you think she had a stalker?"

"No. I don't think so. I think she would have told somebody."

"Okay, that's it Michelle. Thank you for co-operating. I'm sorry for your--"

"Hold on."

"Yes?"

"Have you checked her Facebook profile?"

"No, why?"

"I don't know. Before Kevin, she dated a lot. She wouldn't have told her mom though. She brought a couple guys around. We had a few double date disasters." She sniffled and cleared her throat. "Anyway, you might want to check for pictures, or messages on there, if you can get into that stuff. I'm sure you can."

"Michelle, could you make me a list of past boyfriends? Guys she was with at some point that maybe stick out to you for one reason or another?"

"Yeah, sure, but they're probably all on Facebook. I don't know most of their last names."

"Just in case. You can bring the list in yourself, or send them to my email address. You've been very helpful."

When he hung up, he started browsing the photos on Facebook that he could view publicly. For a while, he found himself clicking through photos of Lisa and Kevin, but further back in her history, there were other men. Several.

He hoped Michelle's list would narrow it down.

As the sun set, he set out for Crown River Park, and wondered what Avery was doing.

He hadn't received any more texts from her, and after seeing her outside class, he worried about her emotional state.

She was always at the back of his mind, just outside the place he allowed himself to focus on, but she was always there.

He wished he could tell her that.

Chapter 22

Moments after Noah arrived at the park, he got a text from Pete.

Come now. South side entr.

On my way. 30 mins.

Noah wanted to call Ethan and let him know something was happening, but without knowing the details, he kept it to himself. He was less than ten minutes away when he got the call from Pete.

"I tried to get him," he was out of breath, " and I almost got him, Cotter."

"Arnold?"

"Yeah, I was circling the park, and flashing my light in and around. I heard a scream, and I bolted. I just went for it and I saw him. Guy in a mask, same as Arnold's. Fit his description for height and weight. He stood—" Pete wheezed, "he stood up from where he knelt over her and ran. I chased him, but he got away on foot. I shot at him. Don't think I got him though."

"You did good Pete," Noah said, " and the girl?"

"It's one of ours. Temple. Lilith Temple."

An image of the woman flashed through his mind. She was new, not as new as Noah, but she had only arrived a few months before. She had been an emergency calls operator, and transferred to be an officer. She was smart, as far as Noah could tell, and tried to make a point to get to know everyone at the department. Not charismatic, not pretty, but kind.

"Is she dead?"

"Yeah."

Noah ran a red light.

"Police there?"

"Yeah, and paramedics."

"I'm almost there. Just stay there, alright?"

When Noah arrived at the park, he ran along the path at the south side entrance until he came to a clearing with picnic tables. Two police officers had begun setting up police tape and the paramedics were packing up.

Pete jogged over to meet him. His dark skin illuminated by the park lantern above.

"I'm sorry."

Noah shook his head and walked toward the scene as the other officer taped it off.

"You did what you could. Don't be sorry."

"She was..." Pete looked over his shoulder at the body, "I think she was still alive when I ran past her."

Noah held his hand up, and looked down at Lilith Temple's body as the red lights flashed across her.

She was in uniform.

"The bastard knew who she was." Pete came to stand beside him over the body. "He knew she was a cop. He's not picking these girls randomly. He did this on purpose."

Her coat had been thrown to the side, and her white collared shirt was slashed twice. Deep parallel cuts ran from under her breasts to her pant line, exposing her rib cage.

"You mean he brought her here?"

Another police car drove down the path with it's cherry's flashing, and the M.E. followed close behind.

"Pete, take me through what happened again, alright?" Noah nodded to the officer taping, and walked back down the path to meet with the others. "I'm lead on the Arnold Henderson case. I'll be right back."

Pete led him back to the south entrance, and they walked to his car a few feet away.

"I was finishing my tenth lap around this place since six," Pete rested his hands on his hips, "I was shining my light in, trying to see if anyone's still stupid enough to be in here after dark. I hadn't seen anyone entering since five. No cars in any of the lots."

"Okay."

"So I shone my light in, and my windows were down, and I heard the scream. A woman. I got out and ran down the path."

"Go ahead."

Pete led him down the curved path. "The screaming stopped when I got here, and I still couldn't see anything."

They sped up. "Then right here, I saw him in his mask. He stood up, looked at me, and that's when I took aim. He started running north and I fired twice. He kept running, so I ran after him."

As they walked, Noah took note of the tree line. No movement.

"I passed Temple and I didn't slow down. Didn't even know it was her. I shouted for him to stop, shot again, but he darted into the trees over there."

"Did you go in?"

"Yeah, I followed him right in."

They jogged to the tree line and Noah shone his flashlight around, searching for blood or footprints.

He took out his phone and called Palfry.

"We need the K9 unit out here now. Arnold was in Birch Falls Park and killed again. He's getting away."

"I'll send the unit now. Stay there." Palfry barked.

Noah hung up and crouched low in the forest. There was no sign of anyone running through and no blood that he could see.

"I let him get away." Pete said.

"No, you did your best Pete. Listen, if you hadn't been here, we wouldn't know this much. I'm glad you were here, alright?" Noah patted his hand down on Pete's shoulder and headed out of the woods. "Let's go."

Pete followed behind him as they hiked back to the scene.

"Why would he bring her here?" Pete asked.

"He's playing with us. Proving he can do whatever he wants and he's getting away with it."

Noah flipped through his messages to the last one he sent Avery, and typed.

There was another murder tonight. A female officer.

"There should have been official detail patrolling through here." Noah's phone buzzed, and he checked it.

Who? Where?

Birch Falls Park. All I can say for now.

"This is on Palfry's head." He slipped his cell in his pocket, "I'm getting twenty-four seven security put on both parks. I don't care what excuses he gives."

"If Palfry's bosses are putting pressure on him for a capture, why wouldn't they okay the security?" Pete asked.

Noah shook his head and looked across the grass at Lilith's body on the path.

"Did you know her?"

"Just a bit, just like most of the department I guess. You?"

"Never talked to her. Too shy."

"You?" Noah smiled. "Come on."

Pete shrugged, but he didn't return the smile. "Do you think he was at the department? Just waiting for a woman to leave?"

"I don't know how he got her," Noah looked around the park, "but he had to have taken his vehicle to get away. The dogs might be able to tell us where he parked."

Pete pointed north. "My bet's that way."

Chapter 23

"I DON'T KNOW WHAT to give you," Charla dumped her whole suitcase out on her bed. "I mean, I know I got this sweater from Maggie and Arnold, but I don't know if he even knew about it, other than seeing me open it. He sure didn't shop for it."

"Okay, that's a good start though." January took the sweater and folded it on Avery's bed.

"I wear this cardigan most often." Avery held it up in front of her before she folded it. "If he's been watching me a lot, I'm sure he's seen me in it."

"Good." January said.

"I wear this necklace all the time." Charla cupped her gold locket in her hand. "My mom and dad gave it to me for my sixteenth birthday."

"Teresa and John?" January asked.

"Yeah. I wear it almost everyday, but..."

"You'll get it back," January told her, "anything either of you want back, I'll make sure you get it again. This is important."

Charla nodded and pulled her hair to the side, while Avery unhooked the chain for her. She let it fall into Charla's hand and she clipped it back together.

"It means a lot to me."

"Good." January said, and Charla handed it to her.

"How are you sending these?" Avery asked. "Or is someone coming for them?"

"I'm taking them." January started for the door.

"Wait, you're leaving?" Avery asked, "what if, when you come back, you lead him to us?"

"I won't be back, actually," January turned around at the door, "I'll be more useful to them there, helping to set this up. Ralph's more useful here. I'll be back with a bag. Anything you think might help, I'll take."

When she left the room, Avery sat down on the bed.

"It's just going to be us and the boys."

Charla picked up a top and shook it out. "Do you think he'll fall for it?"

"Arnold? I don't know. They're putting a lot of detail into this. He's still in Birch Falls, or close to it, meaning he's at least two hours away from us."

"How do you know?"

"There's been another death..."

Charla turned around and sat down. "Tonight?"

Avery nodded.

Charla opened her mouth, but closed it again, and picked up another shirt. "Maybe he's moved on then. Maybe he doesn't care where we are."

Avery hadn't considered the possibility. "I think he was going to go after Fiona no matter what because she got away. Then, when he heard about me, he had us both taken to the forest. Since I survived, and found out he was still free, I've assumed he's coming for me."

"Do you think he's coming for me?"

Avery hadn't thought about that either. "They are keeping you here for your protection, so maybe."

"Doesn't really answer my question."

They heard footsteps down the hall, and January came back to the room with a duffel bag.

"If you need anything, you know to just ask Ralph or Blue, right?"

"Yeah." Avery tossed her cardigan in the bag. "Will you let us know right away? If you get him?"

"Of course." January added the last shirt, zipped the bag, and threw it over her shoulder.

"You're going now?" Charla asked.

"Yeah, they want to set it all up for tomorrow. We can't wait any longer."

Charla walked over to her. "Be careful."

"I will--" January started, but Charla wrapped her arms around her.

"You guys will be fine." She smiled and pulled away. "I feel bad I'm leaving you with the boys. I think Louie's the most well-behaved out of the lot."

"January?" Charla said. "If he knew I was his daughter, do you think that would make a difference to him?"

January pressed her lips together and sighed. "I couldn't tell you that. I don't think anyone could but Arnold himself. You'll be able to see him if you want, once we catch him. You could ask him then, but who knows if he'd tell you the truth."

"Right..."

"Charla, I don't want to hurt you, but if I had to guess, I'd say he'd kill you too. You're the same age as most of his victims, and he doesn't have an issue with killing family members. I'm saying you can't trust him, alright?"

Charla nodded. "I know that."

"Okay. I'm off guys. Hopefully, I'll be seeing you back home soon." January rested her hand against the door. "Watch out for each other."

"We will." Avery sat back down on the bed as January disappeared from the doorway.

"Good luck." Charla whispered under her breath.

Chapter 24

"You got the clothes?" Noah asked.

"That and more," January said, and Noah heard the lack of punch in her tone.

"Ken?" Ethan said. "What have ya got for us?"

"The security cams are ready. House on the border of Crown River and Birch Falls. New development. Only home on the street that was move-in ready."

"Construction?" Noah asked.

"During the day yes, but not on that house. On another part of the division."

"We told you to find a more isolated spot." Ethan said. "Come on, Ken."

"I tried," Ken threw his hands up and looked at Noah, "this was the best I could do on short notice."

"What is it? The show home?" Ethan groaned.

"It was." Ken said. "I convinced the owner to build a new one."

"Fine." Ethan coughed, "Noah, work with it."

"As soon as January gets here, we're going over the plan with Palfry, and moving out." Noah went to the dry erase board. "This, here, is where we set up. Then one car here," he circled a car down the street, "and one here. Ken, get this image to Ethan."

The other mark was on the main road outside the subdivision. "We use someone's driveway. We'll know who goes in and out."

"How about there?" Ken pointed to the subdivision behind it.

Noah made another mark. "Yes. Good?"

"Keep the girls away from the windows in the daylight." Ethan said. "Who's staying in the house with them?"

"January and Pete Thompson," Noah said. "I'll be coming and going once each night."

"You think he'll take the bait?" Ken asked.

"I doubt he'll be able to resist." Noah turned back to the board. "He doesn't get in the house. Period. We take him before he goes in. We have all the proof we need."

"Noah, I spoke to Palfry. He needs to sign off on all these decisions, but I'm behind you, alright?"

"Thanks Ethan. We just need the girls to arrive and--"

"Who did you get?" Ethan asked.

"Hinton and Young."

Silence filled the room.

"I can see it." January said. "Hinton looks a bit like Avery. Blonde."

"From a distance I guess," Ethan said. "Charla and Young, they've both got those curves..."

"You've been checking out their curves?" January asked.

"Who wouldn't notice Jennie's curves in all the right places?" Ken laughed. "Am I right?"

"Alright, that's enough." January said. "I think the clothes will help. They'll be a perfect fit for both. I also got a necklace Charla wears all the time, so Young will need to make sure it can be seen."

"This is a fine line to cross between having him think he recognizes them and having him see it's not them. We need him to see their figures, their shapes..."

"How can you miss Jennie's shape?" Ken laughed, "Am I right?"

"Enough, Ken." January said.

"What? Gimme a break. I'm trying to lighten the mood."

"You want to focus on her looks and--"

"That's what we're supposed to be talking about! Come on, January, you jealous?"

The door opened and January stepped in with a duffel bag over her shoulder. Her hair was flat and her clothes were wrinkled, but Noah smiled when he saw her.

"Good to have you back." he said.

"Speak for yourself." Ken focused on the computer screen again.

"We're so close," Ethan mumbled.

Ken waved Noah over to the screen.

"Ken's got the surveillance outside the department up. Lilith Temple is seen leaving the building at..." Noah searched for the time, and Ken pointed to the bottom corner of the screen. "Seven thirteen. She goes to get in her car, and--"

"What?" Ethan asked.

January came around the table to watch, and Noah made room.

"Arnold, with his mask on, grabs her and pulls her into a van. A black van. Different from the truck he took to *The Sweet Grass* to kill Beelson. Lilith fought him, but they're driving off now at seven fourteen. Less than a minute from when she left the building." Noah leaned on Ken's chair. "He heads west with her, toward Birch Falls Park, and he's the driver. No one else with him that I saw."

Ken and January shook their heads. "He was alone."

"So he waited for her?" Ethan asked. "Knew what time she got off?"

"I reviewed the tape from when Arnold arrived. No other women left the department until Lil." Ken said.

"So maybe he didn't care who." Noah said. "But he had to know we'd see this."

"She was sweet." January stepped back from the screen.

"I didn't know her well," Ken said, "but she introduced herself to me. We've talked a few times."

"Yeah, same." Ethan said. "Listen, let's get this operation set, and call me when you leave Noah."

"Got it."

They hung up and January checked the hall for Hinton and Young. "Not yet. No sign of Palfry either."

"How were the girls when you left?" Noah asked.

"Good, probably better than they've been since we got there."

"Good." Noah said. "You okay?"

"Yeah." January smiled until Ken stood and she crossed her arms. "Let's ride in separate cars."

"Fine." Ken said. "I'm going to go set up the cams."

"Thanks." Noah nodded and Ken grabbed his packs. "Make it look like you're sneaking around. Just in case."

"Will do." Ken said.

When he left, January sat down in her usual seat. "He drives me crazy. I thought it was going to be nice to get out of that house, but I forgot I was coming back to him."

"You sure nothing's wrong?" Noah asked.

"Just feel bad about leaving the girls I guess," she shrugged.

"Why?"

"Blue doesn't talk much," her lips formed a soft smile, "and Ralph's not that easy to talk to either."

"How are Avery and Charla getting along?"

"They're working some things out."

"That's good, right?"

January smiled and raised her brow. "It's best not to try to understand their relationship. They don't yet, either."

"Gotcha." Noah looked at the dry erase board. "What do you think?"

"I think we're going to catch a killer."

Chapter 25

Avery reached under her pillow and checked her phone again. Still no response from Sadie.

She texted her the night before to let her know she was safe, and that she wanted to talk about how her first day back to class went. She usually got a response back within an hour.

Her phone vibrated and a text from Josh flashed on the screen.

Veronica says hi. Snoopy got adopted.

Her lips spread into a smile as she recalled the overfed beagle that was brought in to the shelter a month before.

Tell Veronica I miss her.

How's Lou?

Good. He's snoring at the moment.

Avery had tucked Louie in his new crate, courtesy of Blue, and pushed the blankets up to make a cocoon for him.

She turned over and saw the empty bed beside her.

Time to get up.

On her way downstairs, she wondered if Blue had a pet of his own, and if he spoiled it the way he did Louie.

The sky out the front bay window was cloudy, and the tree leaves rustled in the wind.

"Did January get back okay?" Charla sat down beside Ralph at the table and rested her chin on her hand.

"Yep."

"Have you heard anything from her yet?" Avery asked.

"Just when she got there. No news yet." Ralph said.

"I think I'm going to try to sleep." Blue went to the couch and sat down.

"There?" Avery scrunched her nose up. "Why not use your bed?"

"Look," Charla pointed to the window, "it's really coming down."

The rain drops tapped against the roof and sprayed across the bay window with the wind.

Ralph's phone vibrated and he brought it to the back door with him. "Hello."

"I wonder if there will be a thunder storm?" Charla went to the window and looked outside. "Think Louie would be scared of thunder and lightning?"

"I don't know." Avery went to the stairs and leaned on the railing to try to hear what Ralph was saying.

"Right," Ralph said, "I will but what…"

Avery struggled to catch the rest, but Blue started to snore.

Charla turned around and covered her mouth with her hand, but a few giggles snuck out.

"Okay, good luck." Ralph walked back down the hall and set his phone on the table.

"Was that January?" Charla asked.

Ralph looked down at Blue. "Charming."

"What's going on back home?" Avery asked.

"Not to worry. They're ready for him." Ralph sat back down at the table and picked up the newspaper.

Please, Avery thought, please don't let him slip away this time.

Chapter 26

"How do they look?" Noah asked. "Everybody in their positions?"

Noah had spent the whole day going over the plan with the team, and explaining things to Palfry for the third time.

Palfry had agreed to everything, as long as he called the shots. Noah did as Ethan suggested and let him have the control.

"They are sitting down to dinner now. Unit one says he can see their shadows behind the curtains. Unit one and two are ready." January said. "You're a go."

Noah slipped his phone in his pocket, walked over to the bar, and handed Joe a fifty dollar bill.

"This should cover the other night too. Sorry about that."

He thought about his last meeting with Darrel and the confrontation they had at the bar. He played their meeting over in his head and each time he changed the way it ended.

He took Darrel somewhere safe. He brought him to a train station and bought him a ticket to go anywhere he wanted.

In each daydream, Darrel lived.

In reality, Darrel bled out on the floor of The Sweet Grass Motel.

Joe smiled and nodded. "I'm not even going to ask. Thanks, man."

"No problem."

"Hey, where's your friend been?"

Noah hadn't tried to contact Owen, but when he thought about his old friend, he wished he could get some advice from him. Or just have a cold beer in each other's company.

Noah shook his head and shoved his hands in his pockets, "Best not to ask about that either."

Joe waved, and Noah took his time leaving the bar and getting to his car across the street. No familiar or suspicious vehicles.

He got in and waited until the road was empty as far as the eye could see before pulling into the traffic. He headed east, turned the radio on, and sat back in his seat.

His stare drifted down to his key chain, and he remembered his drive with Avery, and telling her about the significance of the pink ballerina his step-niece had given him.

She told him she believed in him, and as they drove down the country road together, into the sunset, he could barley take his eyes off of her.

He dropped her off that evening, and it wasn't until he found her at Tipper's Point that he saw her again.

Cold, dirty, bloody, and scared.

He wondered if she was scared now, and thought about holding her in his arms. About making her feel safe.

For a while, he felt like he was really driving to see Avery.

His cell phone rang.

Palfry.

"On your way?" he boomed and Noah could tell he was smiling.

"That's right, just left the bar."

"Good."

Noah was sure January had given him an update, but Palfry *had* to bother him, had to know from him what was happening. Noah was surprised Palfry hadn't insisted on coming with him.

"I'll let you know when I arrive."

"Good."

Palfry hung up and Noah dialed January again.

"Palfry just called." he said.

"You too?"

"Listen, I'm about fifteen minutes out now. Make sure to keep alert until I get there."

"We're ready."

Noah hung up and dialed Ethan's number.

"It should've been both of us." Ethan said when he answered. "I should have been in that car with you, catching that son of a bitch."

Noah pictured him in his hospital bed.

"I'm sorry."

"You've got nothing to be sorry about. You'll be sorry if we don't nail him within a week, I'll tell you that though." Ethan said. "You see him, you get him at *all costs*. You got me?"

"I do."

Noah hung up and was unsure if Ethan truly meant the extreme he alluded to.

Dead or alive.

Noah was close to the subdivision, and he knew Unit Three was parked along the road, but he couldn't see them.

Good.

His phone rang. January.

"Unit three saw you drive by."

"Pulling into the subdivision now. Just like we planned."

He pulled up to the show home at the end of the well paved road. Another road behind it led into another new build between the safe house and the older northern subdivision. He pulled into the driveway and while he waited, he called Palfry.

"Here."

"Good. Any sign of him?"

"Not yet."

"Call me if there is."

Noah got out of the vehicle and opened the trunk. He threw the purple duffel bag over his shoulder and looked around before he climbed the steps to the front entrance.

His cell phone rang when he got to the door and he answered.

"Hold your position." January said. "Suspicious truck pulled into the subdivision past Unit's Three and Two."

Noah heard the engine in the distance behind him. It slowed down along the rocky street that formed a T with the one the girls were on. The truck was black, the street was dark, and Noah give it more than a glance over his shoulder. The truck stopped at the bottom of someone's driveway, just out of view.

The front door to the house opened and Pete stood at the door.

"You think he'll recognize me from the park?" he asked.

"Give it another second," Noah said, "and then open the door a little wider."

"It's a male, that's all I can see." Pete said.

"Now." Noah handed him the duffel bag and Pete swung the door open. "Girls still in position?"

"Yep." Pete said.

"Okay, this is enough. I'm going in." Noah said. "If there's even a chance it's him, I'm taking it. Tell Unit Two to follow my lead."

"Good luck." Pete shut the door as Noah turned back.

He went down the steps and casually looked toward the vehicle.

Still running. Still in the same spot.

Noah got in his car, and when he looked in the rear view mirror, the truck made a U-turn and started back out toward the street.

"Unit Three," Noah called, "we've got the potential suspect exiting the subdivision."

"Should we stop him? Tail him?"

Noah called Ethan on his cell.

"Potential suspect exiting subdivision. Ethan, I'm going to follow it."

"Copy that."

Chapter 27

Avery stared out the window as the rain whipped in every direction. "I wonder if there's a storm where they are?"

"Probably." Charla finished the dishes and hung the tea towel to dry.

Blue paced the room and checked out the front and back windows every few minutes.

"Something wrong?" Ralph asked.

"Red hasn't checked in."

The lights flickered off, on, and off again.

"This is not a test." Blue said. "Go to your room with Ralph."

Ralph stood so fast, he knocked his chair over. "Follow me."

Chills raced up Avery's back.

Something was wrong and every part of her body told her to run— not walk.

They followed behind Ralph as he climbed the stairs. Avery looked over her shoulder and Blue had a hand gun out. A crash from the back door made Avery jump and she hurried to catch up with Ralph and Charla as they ducked into the bedroom.

They heard a gun shot, and Charla screamed.

"Quiet now." Ralph closed the door behind them.

Avery went to the crate and grabbed Louie in his blankets. He licked Avery's chin, and she held him tight to her chest.

"Stand by the window." Ralph gestured with his gun, and they stood with their backs against the wall.

Ralph aimed his gun at the door, and they heard another shot fired before Ralph turned to them.

"Push the beds against this door when I leave. You go out that window," he reached into his pocket and pulled out a key chain, "just take the car and go. Don't look back."

Avery took them and nodded.

Charla grabbed one of the mattresses and pulled it to the door. Avery set Louie down and grabbed the other side to the door.

Ralph opened the door, slipped out, and dragged it against the door. As they stacked the second mattress, another shot rang out.

"We should go now." Charla whispered.

Avery nodded. "Open the window."

Charla went to the window and Avery grabbed Louie. As Charla struggled to take the screen out of the window, Avery heard someone on the staircase.

And whistling.

"It's him."

The words caught in her throat, and tears formed in her eyes.

Charla started to shake as she yanked at the screen. It came lose in her hands and crashed to the floor.

The whistling stopped outside the room.

Avery held Louie out to Charla. "Go first. I'll buy us time."

Charla shook her head, and pushed Avery to the open window. "Go. I'll be right behind you."

Avery started to climb through the opening and realized how hard it would be with Louie in her arms.

"Uncle Arnie?" Charla called as Avery slipped out the window, and the words made her stomach churn.

She wanted Charla to follow behind her, but she knew she needed more time to get down from the roof and start the car. She slid toward the edge with Louie tucked in her arms. They were soaked by the time her legs dangled off the edge.

She couldn't hear Charla's voice anymore as she looked down at the ground and willed herself to jump.

Chapter 28

Noah had Ken run the black truck's plates, and the owner had no priors. If Arnold stole the truck from him, he should have reported it missing, but there were no reports, or any irregularities regarding the vehicle.

The further south Noah went, the more he felt something was wrong.

"The truck belongs to a Gregory Dalton, who resides in Toronto. The truck seems to be heading home."

"Well keep following it." Palfry groaned. "If you don't know who's driving, you won't know until they stop."

"Permission to pull the truck over, sir?"

"No." Palfry hung up and Noah called January.

"Hey, listen, this doesn't feel right."

"I know. I just called Ralph, but no answer."

"Something's not right." Noah said. "I think this is a wild goose chase. Keep trying to get Ralph on the line, and I'm pulling this truck over."

"Okay."

"If you can't reach him, send a police unit from North York over without their cherries on."

When he hung up, he put his lights on, but the truck ahead continued.

"Ethan," he said when he answered, "something's not right. I'm pulling him over."

"What do you mean?"

"January said Ralph isn't answering his cell, but I know they spoke not too long ago."

"Alright, keep me on the line." Ethan said.

The black truck pulled over to the side of the highway, and the third unit pulled over to the side in front of it.

Noah got out of his car, and walked over with his phone in his pocket. He let his right hand hover over his gun as he approached, and he grabbed it when he got to the window.

A man's face appeared as he rolled the window down, and his picture matched that of Gregory Dalton.

"License and registration please." Noah said.

"I'm sorry officer, was I speeding? I didn't think I was."

He handed Noah his information.

"Why were you down at the new development in Crown River tonight?" Noah asked.

"My wife and I bought a house there. I was just checking to see if they were on schedule, and if we'd be in by Christmas this year."

"Are you aware that you're not allowed on that property?" Noah asked. "Did someone tell you to go there?"

"No sir. I know we're not allowed, but I figured it couldn't hurt."

"Alright," Noah handed him back his papers, "drive safe."

He waved off the third unit, jogged back to his car, and pulled his phone out of his pocket.

"It's not him." Noah heard a beep, and connected January on the other line, "January?"

"Still no answer from anyone. I called the local police, and they've been informed of the situation. They're sending someone there immediately."

"To the safe house?" Ethan asked.

"Right. No answer from Blue or Red either."

"This truck wasn't a decoy," Noah said, "the guy checks out and no one told him to go there."

"Okay, let's wait to hear from your contact in North--" Ethan started.

"January, text me the address." Noah said. "I'm going."

"I'm going too." January said.

"No, this hasn't been okay'ed by Palfry." Noah said. "I'm not having you lose your job over this, January. I'm already half way there."

"You're not okay'ed either," Ethan said, "and if something is wrong, you won't get there in time. You could blow everything if this is a false alarm."

"I'm going. I'll deal with Palfry later." Noah hung up, and continued down the highway.

⤴

"Uncle Arnie?" she heard herself repeat the words, and tried to remain in control of her body as it shook.

"Charla?" His voice came from behind the door. "Let me in."

"I can't." She raised her voice. "You know I can't. Why are you doing this?"

"Let me in." He yelled, and banged on the door as she backed away to the window.

She watched Avery trying to maneuver herself over the edge of the roof with Louie tucked under her arm. Charla knew she could jump it.

She would have to jump it.

The door opened a sliver more each time Arnold banged on it.

It was Arnold, she thought, as she watched Avery's head disappear, and hoped she hadn't fell.

No mask. Just his unshaven face.

"Charla?" his voice seemed calm. "Come on, you know I don't want to hurt you."

She leaned against the window, and while her body was getting ready to climb out, her mind wanted to stay and talk with her father.

"You killed everyone." Charla said. "You killed mom and dad and Aunt Maggie."

"I'm sorry you had to see that, Charla. Your home should be your safe place."

The softer he spoke, the more she shook.

"You ki-killed them."

"They turned on me," he said and his voice sounded like the man she remembered, "but I just wanted Maggie to come back home with me. I just wanted things to be how they were before. Don't you want to go back home, Charla?"

She steadied herself against the window frame. "We can't go back."

"We could, Charla. You and me. You won't turn on me? Will you Charla?"

That was it. He was playing a game with her and she knew it.

She jumped through the window as a loud bang sounded behind her.

She didn't look back, and focused on the jump ahead. She slid to the edge, and without thinking, turned back to the window.

Her father stood at the window and stared down at her.

Charla jumped off the roof and landed in a crouched position on the muddy grass. She couldn't see Avery, so she ran.

She ran around the front of the house, and saw bright headlights shine toward her.

The grass and mud made her slip, and without traction, she felt like every stride would send her to the ground. As she approached the car, Avery opened her door and stuck her head out.

"Run!" Avery screamed over the rain, but she wasn't looking at Charla. She was looking at the house.

Charla looked over her shoulder and watched Arnold burst through the front door.

Chapter 29

Noah sped down the highway with his siren on the whole way. January texted him the address, and although he received several incoming calls from Palfry, he ignored them.

He kept wondering what the odds were that a man in a black truck would show up at their decoy safe house on the exact night they set up there.

Not unusual or unlikely.

He thought about the odds that something bad had happened at the real safe house, and those odds increased.

For something to happen, for Arnold to know where the safe house was, and attack it on the same night they set up their decoy.

Those odds were slim.

How could he have known where they were? Why would he attack on that night? Had he just found out where they were or did he know more?

Arnold had been in Birch Falls Park twice that past week and killed twice.

Why wouldn't he have been there to kill again? To try to kill another officer and taunt them. Tell them he could get to whom ever he wanted.

Until he got caught by Pete.

If Noah had been at Birch Falls instead of Crown River, he wondered if he could have stopped Lilith from dying, or caught Arnold.

His phone rang, and January's name flashed across the screen.

"What have you got for me?" Noah asked.

"Nothing yet." January said. "How far are you?"

"Ten kilometers out."

"You're in deep shit, Noah. Palfry keeps calling me, asking me where you are."

"Did you tell him where I'm going?" Noah asked.

"No."

"Thank you. I'll let you know when I get there. You let me know what's happening when you can."

He remembered asking Pete to watch over Birch Falls Park.

He hadn't told anyone what he asked Pete to do.

No one knew Pete would be there.

He lingered on the fact as his phone rang,

January again, but he didn't answer.

Arnold would have tried Birch Falls again if he didn't think anyone was going to be there.

But how could he know any of it?

He felt paranoid, but there was only one reasonable answer.

Someone who knew their plans must have told him.

Chapter 30

CHARLA RAN TOWARD THE CAR, but Avery knew she wouldn't get there in time. She knew it the same way she knew what would happen if Arnold got his hands on either of them, and that's when she made the decision.

Avery put the car in drive, turned the wheel toward Arnold, and pressed her foot on the gas.

Through the rain pouring onto the windshield, she saw the figure appear, and time seemed to slow down.

The front of the car hit Arnold, and Avery kept her foot on the gas until the car rocked back as it slammed against the house.

She gasped for breath, as the sound of the pelting rain filled her head.

"Avery!" Charla knocked on the car window, but Avery had locked the doors, and rested in a groggy stupor. "Avery!"

She turned to Charla and tried to catch her breath as she unlocked the door. Her chest ached and for a moment, she thought she was going to die.

As Charla opened the door, Avery watched as the windshield wipers swept the rain and blood back and forth.

"Avery! Here!" Charla started to pull her out of the car.

Avery looked back at Louie as he scratched at the window.

"Louie," she gasped.

"He's okay. Come on."

Avery nodded, stumbled out, and slammed the door behind her to keep Louie in.

Charla held her arm and led her to the front of the car.

Avery expected to see Arnold pinned between the car and the house, but his body laid off to the side, in front of the bay window.

"Is he dead?" Avery asked.

"I don't know."

They stared at the body as the rain soaked them.

Charla shook her head. "We have to go for help. He told us not to come back."

"Louie." Avery grabbed him from the car and held him tight as they staggered to the road.

Charla held onto her arm, and when Avery looked back, he was still lying there.

Her legs felt weak, and although Arnold was still in one piece as far as she could tell, the feeling of impact stuck with her and made her sick.

"I think I killed him." Her stomach rumbled and she bent over.

Avery looked over her shoulder, but from their angle, the body was hidden behind the car.

"Just focus on Louie, okay?" Charla pulled her up.

There was one turn before the main road, but before that was the car stationed by the corner.

The one that Red sat watch in.

In the distance they saw a police car screech around the corner with its lights flashing.

"Help's coming." Charla continued to walk toward it, and waved her arms.

Avery was fixated on the awkward angle Red's head rested against the back of his seat.

"He got Red." Avery held Louie tight to her chest.

The police car swerved to a stop in front of them.

"You have to call Inspector Noah Cotter." Avery shouted to him when he opened the door. "Crown River."

"I was told there might be a problem at the house." The officer yelled over the storm. "What happened?"

"Arnold Henderson broke in. He found us. He tried to kill us." Avery shuddered from the cold.

"Get an ambulance." Charla yelled. "They're all at the house."

"There's back up on the way." The officer said. "Are either of you hurt?"

They shook their heads and the officer walked backwards to Red's car, turned toward it, and said something into his radio that Avery couldn't hear over the wind and rain.

They heard ambulance sirens in the distance, and both girls started to shake.

"Get in." He opened the back door of his car.

Charla went to get inside, but Avery shook her head. "Call Inspector Noah Cotter."

"Please, it's cold out here, you need to warm up."

Avery shook her head and put her arm around Charla.

The first ambulance came and the officer waved it down the road.

"Avery come on, let's just sit in the car." Charla's teeth chattered.

Another ambulance stopped in front of them, and the paramedics hopped out.

"You girls okay? Anyone hurt?"

Charla shook her head, the officer's radio crackled and he stepped away.

The woman wrapped a blanket around each of them.

"Okay." The officer stepped back, and addressed the paramedics. "They need you down there. Two live ones."

The paramedics took off down the road and Avery wrapped her blanket around her front to shelter Louie.

"Listen ma'am," the officer said, "you're in shock. I'm going to--"

"Noah." Avery whispered, and they turned around as a black car sped toward them with flashing lights on the roof.

The officer held his hand out and signaled for Noah to stop, but instead, he drove right up to them.

"He's the inspector on our case." Charla hollered.

Noah jumped out of his car and ran over to them.

"Are you alright?"

Charla looked to Avery, as the officer spoke.

"I think she's in shock."

Avery ran into his arms, and felt them wrap around her blanket.

"You came." Her teeth began to chatter, and her whole body shook violently.

Louie was sandwiched between them, and for the first time, Avery felt warm.

"I'm here, "Noah held her tight and whispered in her ear. "Everything's going to be alright. You're safe, Avery."

Chapter 31

AVERY AND CHARLA INSISTED on coming with Noah, back to the house.

Noah hesitated initially, but decided it would be best to keep the girls where he could see and protect them.

They rode in the back of his car, and as they approached the driveway, an ambulance pulled out. Its sirens wailed and two more paramedics rolled another body toward the ambulance.

He jogged to them and left the girls in the back. "Inspector Cotter from Crown River. Who've you got?"

"We have to get him to the hospital now." They hoisted him up into the ambulance, and Noah recognized Arnold's face.

"The other unit, who do they have?"

"A Ralph Nichol."

"I have to come with you. This man is wanted for several murders."

"Let's go." They slid Arnold into the back.

Noah nodded as they began to hook him up to something.

"Avery," he shouted, "Charla. It's him. I have to go with him."

Charla nodded, but Avery just stared.

"Okay."

"January will be along soon." Noah hollered. "Ride with the other officer to the hospital."

They both nodded and Noah hopped into the ambulance.

"No vital signs." The woman yelled.

Noah pulled out his cell phone and called Ethan.

"I'm in an ambulance with Arnold. He's not responsive. The girls are safe. Ralph's on his way to the hospital too."

"What about Blue and Red?"

"I don't know. I think he killed them."

"Listen, you stay with Arnold, and I'll be down there. January's on her way. Don't let him out of your sight."

"I won't. You're coming down?"

"Hell yeah. Someone's gotta be there when shit hits the fan with Palfry. I'll see you soon."

Noah hung up and watched the paramedics work on Arnold.

They arrived at the hospital, and Noah ran with the paramedics to the nurses, and from there to the E.R.

"This man is a wanted killer." Noah told the doctor, "Where he goes, I go."

The doctor opened the door to the O.R. and Noah followed behind.

The nurse's words muddled together and a wave of relief washed over him as he realized it was over.

Whether Arnold lived or died, he couldn't hurt anyone else again.

Chapter 32

NOAH SAT WITH AVERY on one side and Charla on the other, just outside the emergency room. After Arnold's surgery to stop the internal bleeding, Noah cuffed him to his bed. When he stepped out into the hallway to check on the girls, he wasn't able to leave Avery alone. The look on her face told him she was reliving the moment when she crashed into him with her car over and over again.

They all stared ahead, towards the entrance to the I.C.U.

"You did the right thing." Noah said.

Avery didn't say anything, but her puppy stirred in her lap, and she patted his head.

"So will he..." Charla started.

"He's going to live. He's in really bad shape though. I doubt he can walk right now. The doctor hasn't told me much. He'll be unconscious for a while longer from the meds," he turned to Avery, "then I need to go back in."

Avery nodded and looked down at her pup. "We'll be okay."

He felt Charla's eyes on him, and when he turned to her, she shook her head slightly, and stared wide-eyed at Avery.

She's not okay.

Noah checked his cell phone again.

Nothing.

"So he's the one." Avery eyes searched his,"he's really the man who attacked me. He's the one who killed Tamara and Wendy. Fiona. He killed Charla's family. He is the killer?"

Noah nodded, and yet in the back of his mind, he heard the same doubts that called to him on the way to North York.

They heard the echo of heels clicking against tile and when January rounded the corner, Charla stood and greeted her with a hug.

"You alright?" January asked, and Charla whispered something to her. "Where is he?"

"In there, still under." Noah nodded to the room.

"Ethan and Palfry are on their way." She looked at the girls. "I'm going to talk to Noah alone for a moment. Then I'm going to get you girls home."

"I don't," Charla started, and for the first time that day, she reminded Noah of Avery, "I don't know where I'd go? I don't have a place to go back to really."

January rested her hand on Charla's shoulder. "We'll figure it out together. Don't worry about that right now."

Charla nodded and sat down beside Avery. January nodded to the room Arnold was in, and Noah opened the door for her.

Arnold laid on the hospital bed, wrapped up; wrist cuffed to the metal side guard.

"You shouldn't have left him in here alone." January whispered.

"It wasn't for long, and I knew he was still under. The doctor told me it would be a while before he woke up."

January shook her head. "We can't take chances like that Noah, come on, you know better than that."

"I didn't want to leave the girls alone. They've been traumatized. Charla watched her dad get hit by a car, and Avery…"

"I know." January studied Arnold. "Shit is going to hit the fan with Palfry."

"Listen, we got him. I don't care what Palfry does to me, and I'll make sure he knows you weren't involved."

"I'm going to sit with the girls."

"Could you stay with them while we question them too? Just stay with them in general."

"Of course."

"Don't take them home or anywhere without letting me know, alright?"

She studied him for a moment. "Sure."

"Where is he?" Palfry's voice echoed down the halls.

"Good luck." January left the room and seconds later, Palfry and Ethan stormed in with a young officer behind them.

"Where is that— " Palfry's face was red. "Cotter, step outside now."

Palfry walked back out, looked at the officer, and pointed to Arnold.

Ethan's arm rested in a sling, but he extended his other out, and fist bumped Noah.

"We got him." He mouthed and nodded his head to the hallway.

Noah led him out and watched Palfry as he spoke to the girls.

"Get these ladies something to eat please," Palfry told January, "but keep them in the hospital. We'll need to speak with you both shortly."

January ushered them down the hall.

"I told you not to--" Palfry started, but Ethan held up his right hand.

"We caught Arnold Henderson, and the first thing you want to do is lecture him?"

"I want to know what you were thinking." Palfry crossed his arms.

"January told me Ralph hadn't checked in, or that he'd tried to, and then hung up. She thought something was wrong and so did I. She couldn't get ahold of them, and we can always reach them. So I went." Noah waited for the blow back.

"What happened when you got there?" Ethan asked, before Palfry could speak.

"Coming down the road, I saw two cars. One was our undercover, Red, and the other was an officer. I knew Red was dead before I even parked. Neck snapped. Avery and Charla were distraught, in shock, and the officer told me two EMS units were down at the safe house. He said two people were sent to the hospital. Our officer, Ralph, and Arnold Henderson. Blue, our second undercover, is dead too."

"Did the girls see what happened?" Ethan asked.

"Not really. They know Arnold got in somehow. Shots were fired and Ralph told them to hop out their window, take the car, and go. That's what they did, except as they tried to leave, Arnold came after them. Avery hit him with Ralph's car."

"Wow." Ethan wiped his shiny forehead. "So they don't know how he got in, or anything like that?"

Noah shook his head. "I haven't had time to go over it in depth with them. They don't even know about Blue and Ralph— but they saw Red. I didn't have time to explain. I had to watch Arnold during surgery."

"So he'll live?" Palfry huffed.

"Yes, sir."

"Alright, I want to talk to Ralph first and then the girls." Palfry nodded. "Then Arnold when he wakes up."

"Ralph just got out of surgery, too. He was stabbed in his stomach. Arnold though," Noah nodded. "Doctor says he'll be awake soon."

"Take me to Ralph." Palfry said. "My officer will stay with Arnold."

When they reached Ralph's room, they found him staring at the ceiling.

"Ralph." Ethan said, and he blinked his eyes. "Ralph, thank God you're alive."

Noah went to his bedside and looked down at him.

"We got him Ralph. We got Arnold."

Ralph smiled up at him and nodded.

Chapter 33

"The power went out, so we knew something or someone set off the perimeter security. January called, but my top priority was the girls, so I took them upstairs, and followed the plan. Blue was downstairs, and we heard a crash. He got in through the sliding glass doors in the back."

Ralph took a deep breath and shook his head. Noah wondered if he was thinking about how Avery stopped him in the end, or how he himself hadn't been able to.

"It's alright, Ralph, just take your time." Ethan stood and went to the door. "Girls aren't back from lunch yet."

"You kept those girls safe. You did a fine job." Palfry nodded. "Go on when you can, Officer."

"I gave the girls my car keys, told them to barricade the doors, and slip out through the window. They weren't to come back. I hoped Red would be up the road." Ralph shook his head and looked up at them. "They were good guys. They couldn't have helped what happened."

Noah nodded.

"We heard gun shots, and when I left the girls, I went downstairs. Arnold was on the floor and Blue had his gun aimed at him. They heard me coming down the stairs, and Blue looked up at me, and Arnold rose up and stabbed him in the chest. It happened so fast. Blue shot again, reflex, and Arnold ripped his knife right down the middle of Blue. I shot at him, but..."

"Go on." Palfry said.

Ralph shook his head. "I'm the reason Blue's dead."

"He took his eyes off the target. That's why--" Palfry began.

"No, I startled him, and then, when I was shooting at Arnold, he used Blue's body as a shield." Ralph pressed his lips together and shook his head. "That's why I couldn't get him."

Ethan walked back to the bed. "Ralph, you did what you were--"

"Officer Nichol," Palfry said, "please continue."

"Arnold threw the body toward me. He picked Blue up and threw him. Blue was a big guy. He's strong. I chased after Arnold, gun drawn, and when I followed him to the back, I noticed the broken sliding door. That's when I felt his knife in my gut." He choked on the last word. "He'd have sliced me down the middle if he hadn't heard the girls upstairs. This is where I get hazy. I reached for my gun, but Arnold kicked it away, ripped the knife from my stomach and marched upstairs. He was calm."

"Calm?" Palfry repeated.

"Joyfully. He was whistling. God, he was happy…"

"He thought he had them trapped." Noah said.

"Thank you for your service Officer Nichol," Palfry nodded, "you will be honored for your bravery."

Noah watched Palfry leave the room. He knew it was their cue to follow.

"The girls are safe because of you." Ethan nodded, "I'll see you before we go, Ralph."

Ralph nodded as Ethan left.

"Cotter?" Ralph looked up at him. "How'd he find us?"

Noah shook his head. "We're working on it. You're a good man, Ralph. You work on getting better, alright?"

"I want to know how he found them." Ethan said when they rounded the corner, and waited at the elevator.

"He must have followed them." Palfry took out his cell phone. "We have to make a statement to the press. Ethan, you'll come with me. Cotter, we'll meet you with the girls. Hear from them, and then Arnold."

He entered the elevator and Ethan followed.

"Shouldn't I come with you?"

Palfry shook his head and looked at Ethan. "Ethan's back as the lead on this case. He's who they'll want to speak with."

The elevator doors shut, and Noah bit his lip.

"Of course." He shook his head and waited for the next elevator.

If January and Ralph weren't followed, he thought, someone from the inside had given Arnold the information, knowingly, or not.

Could it have been someone on the team? Could Pete Thompson have a connection to Arnold? Could it have been someone else from the department?

Noah thought about who he could trust as he rounded the corner.

Ralph was a victim of Arnold's, but he had survived, by luck, or because he was working with Arnold? Had Red or Blue been working with him and been double-crossed?

"Noah." January waved him over. "How's Ralph?"

Both the girls stared up at him. "January just told us."

"He's fine. He's going to be okay. Palfry and Ethan are making a statement to the press now. I guess Ethan's back."

Could it have been Ethan?

"Yeah. Well, glad to hear he's alright."

Noah nodded. "We'll be talking to the girls next."

"I'm going to try to take a nap until you need me." Avery said, and wandered into the waiting room behind them with the pup following close behind.

Noah watched Louie divert off course, and pull his leash toward a therapy dog coming from a patient's room.

"Louie," Avery called, "no."

"You know that dog needs a blue collar to be in here, right?" The woman holding the other dogs leash gave Avery a confused look.

"It's alright." Noah held up his badge.

The woman gave it a quick look and led her dog down the hallway. "Come on, Coco."

Louie continued to pull Avery in Coco's direction, but Avery held him back, and Coco didn't give him a second glance.

"Okay, right, you should get some rest too Charla."

Charla stared up at him, but didn't move. "I can't sleep."

"I need to talk to January. Could you sit with Avery? Keep her company?" Noah asked.

Charla nodded, and they watched her through the glass, as she took a seat beside Avery.

"They took it hard— about Blue. He was so good to Louie."

"I have to tell you something while we're alone." Noah said, and January turned to face him, "This stays between us."

January nodded. "What's going on?"

"I think someone else has been working with Arnold. I don't feel like this is over and I think the girls are still in danger."

Chapter 34

Noah wondered if January was the right person to share his secret with, but when it felt like there was no other option to keep the girls safe, he knew he had to open up to her.

To trust her.

She had taken care of the girls as soon as she met them, and she could have hurt them or given them to Arnold many times over.

It wasn't enough, he thought, to lay everything on the line in regular circumstances, but for now— it had to be.

"You're right, it doesn't make sense." January whispered, as a nurse passed by. "How else could he have known where the safe house was?"

"Palfry suggested you were followed." Noah said. "Doesn't make sense though. Why wouldn't he have attacked on the way? Or anytime before now?"

"We weren't followed. I know we weren't." January glanced over at the girls. "It happened after I left though, Noah. Maybe Arnold killed those women in Birch Falls to set us up to set him up?"

"You think he knew about that? About our decoy house?"

"Yes, don't you?"

"I guess so. Listen, I feel paranoid right now. I don't know who to believe. Palfry, Ethan, Ken, Ralph, Blue, Red, you and I were the only ones who knew the location of the safe house in enough advanced time for Arnold to be able to attack when he did. It's a lot right there, but then add Avery and Charla. We need to check their cell phones and emails. We have to make sure they didn't tell anyone."

"I'm sure they didn't," January said, "but I'll check and make sure."

"I doubt they did either, but something could have slipped from any of us. Even by accident. That's where we start. With these people, and Pete Thompson."

"Pete?"

"I met him at Jennifer Hornby's home after she committed suicide. He was also waiting at the trailer for Palfry and I to come and check it out. I was the only one who went, and it was right after Palfry denied us around the clock security on the parks, so I decided to take matters into my own hands. I told Pete to watch over Birch Falls Park the night Lilith Temple was killed. I was going to watch Crown River

Park, and I didn't tell anyone about Pete. She was attacked on his watch."

"So he could be in on it."

"No one else knew he'd be there; they could have told Arnold it was clear, so he might not be in on anything at all, but we have to account for that. He didn't catch Arnold."

"Right." January rubbed her red lips together. "What do we do?"

"I need you to look out for the girls. Keep them with you at all times and make it discreet. Make it seem like their idea. Like they need you."

January nodded. "I will."

"I'll talk to Avery, and make sure she knows I think it's in her best interest. It's the only way to make sure they're protected."

"How do we figure out who's working with Arnold?"

"It could be small. Arnold could have found out the information on his own, like I said, if someone did it accidentally. If that's the extent of it, we have nothing to worry about. If not, then the best chance we've got is to get Arnold to tell us."

January squinted at Noah. "You think he'll just tell you how he knew about the safe house?"'

"Now that he's caught, he might flaunt it." Noah shrugged. "Or maybe I'll have to trick him into telling. Right now, he's our best shot."

"Why are you trusting me with this?" January asked. "Because I'm already close to the girls?"

"I might be naive. I didn't really have a choice. I can't do this on my own."

"Well, I'm not working with him. I'll tell you that and hope you can take me at my word. I know we don't know each other very well— " She stopped when Palfry's voice could be heard from down the hallway.

"You keep them safe." Noah nodded. "If I get a call from you, just a few rings, and then hang up. I'll know something's wrong."

January nodded.

"We just spoke to the doctor, " Ethan said as they approached, "and as soon as Arnold is stable, we'll transfer him to Crown River Health."

"Why?" Noah asked.

"It's closer to prison, Cotter. Less chance of Arnold escaping when we transfer him." Palfry looked to January. "The girls ready?"

January nodded. "I'll get them."

"Actually, we'll just go see them. Let's go."

January snuck a look at Noah. They followed them into the waiting room, and sat across from the girls.

Avery woke up and sat up straight. Charla crossed her legs and rested her hands in her lap.

"Ladies," Palfry said, "I know you've been through a lot, but we need to hear what happened in your words."

"Actually," Charla looked at Palfry directly, "I want to speak to my dad."

Palfry's mouth opened and his jaw hung. Noah was surprised as well, but he savored the look on Palfry's face before looking back to Charla.

"Why, might I ask?" Ethan asked.

"He's my dad, and I have a right to see him as his family member. As his daughter."

"We cannot let you see him. He has been arrested on charges of murder. He is a danger to all. You should know that." Palfry stared her down.

"May I talk to Charla alone?" January asked.

"Anything anyone wants to say can be said here." Palfry didn't look away from Charla. "No secrets here."

"Charla," January spoke in a soft tone, "I understand you have questions, but your safety is important. We are looking out for your well-being. Then, there's protocol."

"I'm not scared of him." Charla crossed her arms in front of her chest.

"It's not about that." Noah said.

"If I can't talk to him, then I'm not answering any questions."

"You will not be able to see him while he is in the hospital. That is final," Palfry raised his voice, "and you'll co-operate with us, or you'll be charged as well."

Charla sat back in her seat and stared at him.

"Avery," Ethan said, "could you please tell us what happened?"

Avery looked at Charla, and then at Palfry.

"My friend, Sadie, she didn't answer my calls or texts. She hasn't for two days now." She looked to Noah. "Can you check on her?"

"I will." Noah sat back.

"Thank you. It started when the lights went out."

Avery told the story, and they listened on.

"I started the car, and I waited for Charla. I saw her coming, but he was too..."

"It's okay, Avery." January nodded.

"Instead of waiting for Charla, I hit him."

"Right," Palfry nodded and smiled at Avery, "thank you for your cooperation. We'll see to it that you both get taken home safely."

"I don't have a home." Charla seethed. "My family was killed by my dad, and I want to see him. It's all I have. It's my right."

"Calm down. You'll have your chance to see him back home, when he's in prison, should you choose to. Then you'll have had a chance to see things clearly." Palfry nodded to January. "Make sure she is kept away from Arnold."

Palfry left the room. Ethan followed him out.

"Stay with January, alright?" Noah stood.

Charla stared at the floor.

Why was she trying to bargain, he wondered, and followed the men into the hall.

"Alright, Arnold's next." Palfry said. "On this one, Ethan will do the talking."

He didn't wait for Noah to respond, and they both started toward Arnold's room.

Noah took a deep breath and followed them in.

Arnold's eyes were closed; his body covered in his blankets. Ethan pulled a chair beside him, where his wrist was cuffed to the bed, and Palfry stood behind him.

Noah stood just inside the doorway, and realized he had officially taken a back seat on the case.

"Arnold?" Ethan said.

Arnold's eyelids fluttered before he opened them fully, and looked at Ethan.

"Arnold Henderson, you are under arrest for the murders of too many people to name. We know you killed them, and you're going down for this, but we can make your time more comfortable if you tell us everything."

Arnold lay there, expressionless.

"Can you hear me Arnold?"

No movement.

Ethan looked back at Palfry and he nodded.

"Arnold, you killed your own family. Do you have anything to say?"

Arnold closed his eyes, and the machines started to bleep faster.

"You can hear me." Ethan said. "If you want to— "

The machines lit up and a nurse scurried into the room.

"Everybody out," She said, and another nurse followed her in.

"Get out of here." She hollered, and Palfry and Ethan stepped back.

As one nurse checked the machines, the other spoke to Arnold, and then left the room.

"Hey," Palfry shouted to his officer outside the door, "you're staying with him, you hear me?"

A doctor walked briskly toward them.

"He stays with him." Palfry shouted to the doctor, and the officer stepped into the room behind him.

They listened outside until some of the bleeps stopped.

"Let's take him back to surgery." The doctor said, and Palfry grabbed the officer on his way out.

"You stay *right* with him."

"Yes sir." The officer nodded, and as the nurses wheeled Arnold out, Noah got a good look at his face.

His eyes were closed.

"Damn it." Palfry looked up at the ceiling. "Ethan, we're going with him. I want you to be the first person he talks to. Let's go."

Chapter 35

Noah watched Ethan walk toward him with a hopeless expression.

"He wants to talk to you." Ethan stopped in front of Noah, and he stood from his chair in the waiting room.

"I'm off the case, aren't I?" Noah crossed his arms.

Ethan shook his head. "Not Palfry. Arnold. He won't talk to us. Only asked for you."

Noah looked down the hall toward his room. "Why?"

Ethan shook his head. "He wouldn't say. Listen, you're not off this case, but you have to learn how to play things Palfry's way. You may not like it most of the time, but if he's on your side, you've got more power. You have to pick your battles with him. You'll learn."

"So..."

"Palfry's sending you in and you're recording it." Ethan slipped a device in his jacket pocket. "We'll be able to hear everything."

Noah nodded and felt his pocket. "Why do you think he wants to talk to me?"

"I think he wants to try to get away with something, and he thinks because you're young, you'll be easiest to pull one over on." Ethan started walking towards the room. "Try to ask a lot of questions, try to find out how he knew where the safe house was. He's followed you before. He thinks he knows you. Prove him wrong."

Noah nodded and Palfry waddled towards them.

"Listen, Cotter, one last chance."

Noah nodded. "Yes sir."

Palfry stepped aside and let him through.

The room was gray and Arnold watched him walk toward his bed. Noah stood beside him and waited.

"Sit down, Inspector Cotter."

Noah wondered if he should hold his place, or do as Arnold asked, but he sat down on the plastic chair beside him.

"You wanted to see me."

"When we first met, when you interrogated me, did you think I was the masked killer?" Arnold was quiet, and his voice cracked when he started to speak, but his deep tone made each word unmistakable.

"Yes."

Arnold looked down into his lap and back up again. "How about now?"

"The game you've been playing is over. You've been caught Arnold."

"*I* have."

Noah knew he was implying someone else, but remembered the mic in his pocket.

"How did you know where to find the girls?"

Arnold pressed his lips together and lifted his shoulders less than an inch.

Noah looked out the window. "How long did you know where they were?"

Arnold lifted his head and looked past him to the door.

"It's just the two of us Arnold."

"I doubt that," his eyes smiled at Noah, "but I have your attention. I also have a way to get us both what we want."

"What makes you think I'm interested in giving you what you want?"

"I know you are, Cotter." Arnold's eyes sparkled up at him. "I saw you talking with Darrel Beelson at that bar the night he died. You were trying to get more from him, but he couldn't give you anything, that's what I assume happened anyway. Because Beelson was dumb."

"I knew you were there. I know you followed him to the hotel that night."

"So did you." Arnold squeezed his fist open and closed, and rested the cuff against the bed rail. "You tried to look out for him."

"You killed him."

Arnold shrugged his shoulders again. "You want to know how I found the safe house. I want to see my niece."

Noah sat back in his chair and shook his head. "You're not getting anywhere near her."

"I see you're trying to look out for her, too. She's the only real family I have left."

"You tried to kill her."

Arnold stared at him and let his chest fall and rise. "I've told you the deal. Take it or leave it. I'm sure you have to speak to your superiors first though."

Noah didn't blink. "If it's a no?"

"I think the deal's worth more to *you* than me."

Arnold turned his head and looked out the window. Noah stood and walked out of the room.

Ethan and Palfry took their ear buds out and stood.

"Did you notice the wording he chose?" Ethan asked. "He said we want to know how he found the safe house. He might have found it, one way or another, on his own. He didn't say who told him."

Palfry nodded. "Ethan was right. He thinks he can manipulate you."

"Do you think he wants to try to hurt Charla?" Noah asked, "Why else would he want to see her?"

Palfry looked at Ethan. "He just wants control. Plain and simple."

"Well, if it's not dangerous to Charla, maybe we should do it." Noah said.

Ethan rested his hands on his hips. "We might gain the information we want, or he might be playing with us. He might not tell us, or the truth could be as I said, he found it himself. Followed them, or overheard something."

"Is it worth it?" Palfry asked him.

"It might be. I want to talk with my team about it. Then we'll come to you and make a decision."

Palfry nodded and smiled. "Take your time. He's not going anywhere. The doctor told me he couldn't get off that bed, even if he wanted to."

Ethan and Noah went back to the waiting room, and January stood when she saw them approach. They moved away from the girls to the hallway, called Ken, and Noah filled them in on what he heard.

"I think we should do it." January said.

"What do you think, Boss?" Ken asked.

"I don't know. I'm on the fence. I don't know if the information is worth it." Ethan swayed his weight from one foot to the other. "He wants to be alone with her. If he tried something, he could hurt her, even in his condition."

"What's his condition?" Ken asked.

"I doubt he can even walk. His arms though, at least the one not handcuffed to the bed...I don't know." Ethan shook his head and rubbed his shoulder under his sling.

"Not to mention the harm this could cause Charla, even if he doesn't try anything. Who knows what he'll say to her?" January looked at Noah, and he wished they had a moment alone to talk.

"I think we should do it." Noah said.

"Ken," Ethan said, "could we set up some sort of video surveillance in the room? It's the only way I'd feel comfortable giving this a shot."

"I could bring cameras. I could even set them up without him knowing." Noah could tell Ken was smiling.

"How?"

"I'll tell you when I get there. I've got to pack, and I'm on my way."

"Get here soon." Ethan said.

"I can be there in less than two hours." Ken hung up.

"I think this is the right decision." January said. "We make sure we've got the upper hand, and then—"

"Don't get too excited. Palfry has to approve it." Ethan turned away from them. "Don't tell Charla until I get back. I'm going to talk to him now."

They watched him walk down the hall.

"Don't tell me what?" Charla poked her head around the corner.

Chapter 36

"I THINK THEY'RE GOING TO let me talk to my dad."

She heard bits of their conversation, but even as she spoke the words, she wondered if she was making it up.

"Honestly Charla, why would you want to?"

Charla pulled on one of her ringlets and let it slip out of her fingers. "I want to know why."

"What if it upsets you?" Avery scratched behind Louie's ear, "What if the answers are worse than whatever you're thinking?"

"I doubt they could be."

"I don't."

"You're not in my position, okay? You don't know what you'd do until you are."

"I think you've forgotten what position I'm in."

"You're right, I shouldn't even be talking to you about this."

Charla started to get up, but Avery touched her arm.

"I'm the one who asked something I shouldn't have. Let's just not..."

Charla nodded and Avery set Louie on the floor. "I think he needs a walk. I need fresh air."

"I could use some air too." Charla waved January over, but she held her finger up without looking back. "They're having a deep conversation."

"Okay, let's say they let you talk to him—"

"I thought we weren't going there."

Avery sighed, "Just hear me out. If you decide to talk to him, what do you want to hear? What could he possibly say that would satisfy— no— make things better?"

"The truth. Whatever the truth is. Everything has been a lie."

"And if he lies?"

"If he lies to me, I think I'll know it. Maybe I'll be as close to the truth as I'll ever get."

Louie jumped up on January as she approached.

"I'm just going to take Louie for a walk if that's okay?"

"Sure. Why don't the three of us go?" January smiled and pushed him off.

As they walked down the hallway, Charla imagined each of the rooms they walked by could be his.

When they got outside, clouds threatened to unleash rain upon them, and they stuck close to the hospital.

"January? I know you said you'd tell me later, but does what you guys were talking about have to do with my dad?"

January sighed. "I'd like to tell you, but I can't right now."

Charla nodded and walked at a faster pace. She stayed ahead of them on the sidewalk.

If she could talk to her dad, she thought, she could understand what made him want to kill her whole family. She knew she could never fully understand his motives, but to hear from him, to know what he was thinking, or why. She wouldn't have to wonder any more.

Wondering was all she had time to do at the safe house, and when she returned to where ever she was going, she wanted a chance to leave it all behind.

"I spoke to Sadie."

"You did?" Avery looked up at her. "When?"

"Not even an hour ago. Just before our meeting. I convinced her not to come here by telling her we'd have you home tonight."

"Will you?" Avery asked.

"I think so. I think I'll be taking you."

Avery smiled and pulled Louie away from trash on the ground. "Thank you for reaching out to her. I thought something was wrong."

She thought about returning home and getting to be with her friends again. While they were at the safe house, she thought about staying in contact with Charla too after everything was over. She wanted to try to be there for her, as someone who understood all the gruesome details without having to talk about it. Someone who knew what she had been through, and could be there if Charla wanted to talk.

After hearing her decision to try to talk to Arnold, Avery knew they would never be able to have a normal conversation again.

"Charla, let's head back." January shouted and Charla turned around to meet them.

January and Charla turned into the waiting room and Avery met Noah at a vending machine just outside.

Noah knelt down and pet Louie as he ran in between his legs.

"How was your walk?"

"Fine." Avery waited for him to stand again, and when they were face to face, she tried to read his. "January said she might be able to take us home soon."

"Yeah, I guess you miss home."

"I don't really have one right now, except I guess I'll stay with Sadie for a while. I just want to see Sadie and Josh again. Give this little guy a real home too."

"I need you to stay with January for a little bit, okay? When you get back."

"Why?"

"Just until everything gets sorted out. Okay?"

"It's bad, Noah. What I'm feeling. Like I'm crashing over and over again."

January passed by and Charla stopped at the machine.

"You okay?" Charla asked.

"I still can't believe Blue…"

"I know." Charla rubbed Louie's head. "This little guy probably misses him too."

Avery nodded and began to tear up.

"Oh Avery," Charla rested her hand on her shoulder, "I shouldn't have said that."

Avery shook her head and wiped her tears away. From the side of her eye, she knew Noah was watching her.

Her face turned red, and she rushed to the bathroom. The cool air hit her, and she shut the door behind her in the last stall, and leaned on the wall.

"It's too much, it's too much," she muttered the words and looked up at the ceiling, "it's too much."

Thoughts of Blue and Fiona swirled in her thoughts, and she replayed their moments together in her mind.

"You wouldn't let anyone close to you." She shook her head and realized she was speaking about both of them. "But I did. I cared about you."

Fiona's weight on her back. The power shutting off.

The breath knocked out of her when she hit Arnold's body.

"Maybe it's better. Maybe you were both right not to let anyone close, because the pain I feel— I can't imagine what your family and friends are going through."

She thought about Sam, and remembered his visit. His heartache over Fiona.

She pictured Sadie and Josh getting the same news.

"I can't, it's too much." Avery spoke in a calm voice and it scared her.

She opened the door and walked to the sink.

"I can't," she shrugged to herself. "I can't."

She splashed water on her face and watched in the mirror as it dripped off her chin.

"I can't." She whispered, with the same eerily calm feeling, and leaned close to the mirror. "Come on, Avery."

She saw a broken girl staring back at her.

"It's going to be alright. Please let it be alright."

Chapter 37

"Palfry heard Ken's idea and it's a go." Ethan said.

"Ken'll be here soon."

"It's smart really." January looked at them. "Ken dresses as a nurse, brings in a pitcher of water, and asks if Arnold needs anything. He'll never suspect the camera."

"I know, don't tell Ken how smart it is though. He'll want a raise." Ethan looked over at the girls. "January, we'll need you to prepare Charla for this. She needs to feel as safe as possible without knowing they will be watched."

"Of course. Helps that she already wants to see him. No coaxing needed." January looked over at Charla, "I hope this doesn't hurt her more."

"Well, we aren't doing this for her," Ethan said, "we're doing it to get whatever potential information he has from him. He loves playing games and stacking the odds in his favor."

Ethan nodded to them and walked back down the hall and around the corner.

"I think Ethan's right." Noah stepped in front of January. "Arnold's not done playing games."

January nodded. "It's our best bet of finding out what he knows. I know this, but I hate the fact that we have to play along. We've caught him."

"I know. Listen, Arnold's in bad shape, but he could still be planning to use Charla as a hostage to get out of the hospital."

"He's cuffed to the bed."

Noah shrugged. "He could break the bed. He's strong. You know what he did to Blue. I met Blue once, and I wouldn't want to mess with him."

January looked over at Charla. "What do we do?"

"The camera's a good start. We need to make sure she stays out of reach. She needs to know that under no circumstances can she come into physical contact with him. Can't even get within an arms reach."

"Right."

"She needs to know she can leave whenever she wants."

January nodded. "If he has had someone helping him, what if they're here?"

"This stays between us, but Ethan's been acting different with me since Arnold was caught."

"Really? I hadn't noticed."

"Maybe it's because you are used to working for him. Maybe I'm making something out of nothing."

"Maybe. Why?"

"He's been distant with me, and I don't know what he wants."

"I'll stay with Avery while Charla's in there in case this whole meeting is a distraction."

"Good." Noah noticed Avery emerge from the bathroom from the corner of his eye.

When she cried, it reminded him of the first time he met her in his office.

She was worried and scared, but more than anything, she wanted to know the truth. He wanted to console her then, without even knowing her, but keeping things professional was important. Still, seeing her cry made him retreat to that awkward feeling of helplessness.

"January, I don't want to say this, but I have to. If you're working with Arnold in any capacity, I'll personally see to it that you go down for this."

January stared at him and blinked several times. "Same goes for you, Noah."

"Good. We need to tell her to make sure Arnold doesn't find out she's his daughter."

"Right. I think we should tell her now."

Noah nodded and followed her into the waiting room.

"Charla, we've talked about it, and you'll be able to see Arnold today."

"Really?" Charla looked up at January and confusion painted her face.

"Yes, but you have to follow our rules."

Charla nodded. "Okay, yeah."

Noah took a seat beside January and she started to tell her the conditions. Charla nodded eagerly, and with each nod, Noah felt more uneasy.

If we're playing right into his hand, he thought, we could lose everything.

He stood, and without a word, went down the hall toward Palfry. He wanted all the officers they could spare outside the hospital room before Charla went inside.

Ready for anything.

Chapter 38

Noah took one step into the room, and Arnold's eyes opened wide.

"Cotter, you're back." His eyes sparkled, "With good news."

"I haven't told you anything yet."

A smile swept across his face. "It's good news for me either way. Let's hope you made the right decision."

"We've decided to let you see Charla."

"Did she say she would?"

Noah noticed his raised his brows. "Took some convincing, but she was willing to work with us."

Arnold studied Noah and squeezed his hand into a fist. "Can we switch wrists now?"

"No."

"I guess I'll quit with the requests while I'm ahead."

"It's not a game, Arnold. These are people's lives you've taken. I hope you remember that when Charla comes in."

"You giving me advice, Cotter?"

"I need to know something now. I need to know that you didn't stumble across the location of the safe house. That you didn't discover the location after digging. I know it, you know it, and I need you to admit it to me."

"I'll tell you what you want to know after I talk to Charla."

"Just tell me you're working with someone. Admit it."

Arnold shook his head. "Charla first."

"Tell me something else then. Tell me why you asked for me."

Arnold's eyes lit up again. "You know why."

"No games, at least just tell me that."

"You're the one who made this happen. The one that got Charla to speak to me."

Noah sat still and looked at him, careful not to give anything away.

"As much as you want to take care of people, like Darrel, Maggie, Jen, Fiona...as much as you tried to protect them, you couldn't. They're dead. As much as you want to protect Avery and Charla, you know you can't, so you choose the truth. You choose to be the inspector over the protector because you think you have a better chance at catching the killer than saving the victims."

Noah shook his head. "You don't know me at all."

"Oh yeah? Do you know much about Avery? About Charla? Know what Avery's weakness is? Know what Charla's most afraid of? I do and I haven't even spoken to Avery. They don't confide in you because you keep your distance. You try to be professional because you're new. You're young. You've got something to prove."

"So you think you can out-smart me? Trick me?"

"No. That's why *they* think I asked for you. I'm telling you, I asked for you because you want to know the truth more than to protect Charla from me. I wanted Charla in here, and you were the only one who wants it more than I do."

"You don't know— "

"Have you ever gone hunting, Cotter?"

Noah remembered having a similar conversation with Darrel Beelson when they were at Bob Pope's cabin. He had told Beelson he only hunted criminals, not animals.

Looking into Arnold's eyes, he wondered if there was a difference. He wondered if he was looking at both.

"No?" Arnold looked out the window. "You'd be a good hunter, Cotter. A natural— that is if you could kill. Have you ever killed an animal before? Have you ever killed a human?"

"I agreed to let Charla speak to you in exchange for—"

Arnold's eyes flitted from the door back to Noah. "You're closer than you think."

"Inspector Cotter," Palfry called from the door.

Noah stood from his chair and looked down on Arnold.

His eyes twinkled up at him and he waved goodbye with his cuffed hand.

Noah walked down the hall and saw Palfry, Ethan, and Ken huddled in a circle with another officer.

"I can have six men here, four security guards immediately, and two officers shortly after." The officer furrowed his brows when Noah walked over.

"This is Inspector Cotter," Ethan stepped back to allow him in, "how did he react?"

"He's happy. Maybe too happy. Maybe we should rethink this." Noah said.

"Oh, come on," Palfry slapped him on the back, "it's already in motion. You fought for it, and now you don't think we should?"

"Maybe we're playing into his hand."

"I suggested that." Ethan sighed.

Or maybe you don't want us to find out you're working with him.

"Ken," Palfry said, "you confident you can get this equipment in there without him noticing?"

"It's tiny." Ken nodded and looked to Ethan. "Microscopic. I'm sure."

"Then we'll have eyes and ears in there." Palfry looked to Ethan."Make the final call."

Ethan looked at Ken, who nodded.

"Yes, we do it."

Noah stepped back out of the circle.

"Alright," Ethan turned to the officer, "get your people together, everyone you have, and be back here on the hour. We put Charla in then."

Noah turned back to the room and thought about what Arnold said.

He wasn't sacrificing Charla in any way.

They would protect her *and* get the truth.

Arnold thought he knew Noah, but Noah could prove him wrong.

Chapter 39

JANUARY AND CHARLA SAT across from each other in the waiting room, leaned in close, and whispered to each other.

A nurse had stopped a older man in a wheel chair, as he pointed to Louie with a smile. Avery lifted Louie up and rested him on the mans lap. The nurse laughed and the man beamed.

Noah walked over to January, and sat down.

"Sorry to interrupt. They said they'll be ready in an hour." Noah said.

January nodded.

"Good." Charla's eyes darted around the room.

"I came to tell you that in my opinion," Noah glanced over at Avery, still occupied with the man, "I don't think this is the best choice for you. I want you to know that I support you either way though."

Charla stared at him and crossed her arms. "Why are you saying that?"

"I want you to be prepared. Sending you in there was a big decision. One that we are all mostly on the fence about. You say you want to see him, and I think that helped us decide, but I want you to know you can change your mind and it will be fine. No one will be mad."

"He can't hurt me, can he?"

Noah looked at January. "We'll have seven men, including me, standing at the door. We'll be ready to intercept if Arnold tries anything."

Charla leaned back in her chair. "Okay, well what else do you think he'll do?"

Noah pressed his lips together and looked at January.

"Well, like we were just talking about," January said, "you have to be careful what you tell him. He could use it against you or us. You have to leave the room if he says anything to make you uncomfortable."

Charla nodded. "I know that, and I would."

Noah cleared his throat. "He might talk in detail about killing your family. About wanting to kill you. About what he did to all those girls..."

Charla clasped her hands together in her lap and her knuckles turned white.

"I'd just leave, if he said that to me."

Noah nodded. "January and I are looking out for you, alright?"

Charla nodded. "I know."

"Okay, I've got to get back." January looked up at him and nodded. "I'll come back when we're ready."

Noah walked by Avery and heard the old man laugh at something her pup did.

He didn't want to interrupt, but he wanted to talk to Avery too.

"Noah?" Ethan called down the hall.

"I let them know."

Ethan nodded. "We are setting up here. Two hallways down. He can't hear us from here. Ken's on his way in with Palfry's officer, and Palfry's requesting clearance 50 meters on either side of Arnold's room. Here."

Ethan sat down on one of two seats behind a table, and pointed to the monitor Ken brought.

Noah sat down. "Should it be working now?"

"When he sets it up." Ethan nodded. "He should be in now. Charla ready?"

"I think so."

Noah heard a pop.

"What was that?" Noah whispered.

Ethan shook his head and as Noah stood, a woman's scream echoed through the halls.

They bolted toward Arnold's room with their guns drawn.

As they ran down the hall, Noah saw a nurse standing in front of the door with her hand over her mouth. Ethan pushed her out of the way, and when they stepped in the doorway, they saw Palfry's officer lying on the ground with a bullet in his head. A bloody pillow laid beside him.

"Get security at all exits!" Ethan shouted.

The nurse nodded and backed away slowly. "Where's Ken?"

"Arnold's got him." Noah shouted, and pointed at a man in a gown in the hall walking with an I.V pole. "Did two men run by here?"

The man shook his head. "Just a man pushing someone in a wheel chair. They were in a hurry, though."

He pointed down the hall, and Noah ran with Ethan behind him on his radio.

Noah turned the corner, and watched a group of nurses get off the elevator. He thought about taking it down, but changed his mind when he heard someone shout down the next hall.

Ethan caught up to him and they ran side by side toward the noise.

A nurse pointed to the stair well. "A man in a gown with a gun. He's going to kill him!"

Noah ran to the stair case and eased the door open with his gun pointed. Ethan stood beside him and they noticed a wheelchair on the next landing on its side.

"You go up, I'll go down." Ethan nodded.

Noah started up the staircase.

"Noah." Ethan called, and Noah ran back down.

Ethan pointed to the blood on the staircase with his gun.

"They went this way."

They followed the blood trail down the stairs to the first floor, where there were two doors.

One exit and the other back into the hospital.

"I'll go this way," Ethan pointed to the door, "and you take the exit."

Noah nodded and took the exit door to his left. He heard Ethan's door close, at the same time he saw Arnold at the end of the emergency exit alcove with a gun to Ken's head.

Chapter 40

"You take care, Louie." The old man smiled up at Avery, and the nurse nodded as she wheeled him away.

Avery walked Louie back over to January with the intention of asking when they could leave, but Charla's expression made her hesitate. Her brows were furrowed, and she listened intently to January.

"...just let me know. Hi Avery, that little old man was so cute."

"He was, yeah. They thought I was part of the program here, with animals cheering up the patients."

January nodded and looked back to Charla. "We're going to leave as soon as you're finished."

"Really?" Avery smiled.

"Not long now." January squeezed Louie's paw, and he scrambled to lick her hand, but January stood, just out of his reach.

Moments later, they heard a woman screaming.

January drew her gun and stood in front of the girls.

"We have to go, now."

"What's happening?" Charla stood.

"I don't know, but I'll keep you safe. You trust me, right?"

Charla nodded, and another scream echoed through the hallway, more distant than the first.

"Come with me." January gestured down the hall, away from the noises.

She looked back at them and they followed.

"Did he get loose?" Charla whispered.

"Should we wait for Noah?" Avery pulled on Louie's leash and January turned around.

She looked at her for a moment, and Avery realized she had called him by his first name.

"Inspector Cotter's trusted me with you both." January said as they reached the end of the hall. "Come on."

She opened the door to the stairway and Charla rushed through.

"What if..." Avery looked back down the hall, but no noise or commotion caught her attention.

"Avery," January grabbed her arm, "trust me."

She pulled her into the stairway, and climbed down to the next landing. The girls followed her, and she opened the door.

They went through, and Avery saw a man she recognized, and pointed.

"That's Palfry," January whispered and shook her head, "come on."

She opened the door to an equipment room and slipped in behind them.

"Why didn't we go to him?" Avery whispered."Find out what's going on?"

"We need to sit tight for a while." January said. "I have my phone. Cotter will call me when it's safe."

"I don't understand." Avery stayed close to the door. "Why are we hiding from Palfry?"

"Cotter told me there might be someone working with Arnold. Someone we know."

"Do you— " Charla closed her mouth and stared at January, "do you think I was just a distraction? So whoever he's working with could get him out?"

January took out her phone.

"Is he...coming for us?" Avery asked.

January typed something into her phone. "We are safe here."

Avery turned back to Charla and mouthed "We have to get out of here, now."

Chapter 41

"Drop your gun, Cotter." Arnold wrapped his arm tight around Ken's chest, but he swayed from side to side.

He won't get far.

"No. I'm not going to drop the gun because you're not going to shoot him."

Arnold chuckled and coughed.

"What's so funny?"

"That after all this time, you think I'd let someone live?"

"If you kill him, you won't be able to get away. Ken's the only reason you're still alive."

Arnold smiled. "I'm going to give you one last chance. Drop your gun."

"Why would you try to leave now?" Noah asked, "You wanted to talk to Charla."

Arnold stared at Noah and whispered something to Ken with a smile.

"It's going to be alright, Ken." Noah called to him, hoping someone was on the other side of the door.

Ken shook his head and Arnold laughed. "Ken's the only reason I'm alive, you're right Cotter, and he'll be the reason you die."

"No." Ken shook his head. "Please."

"I'm not letting you out of here." Ken's legs shook. ""You took an opportunity to try to escape, but it won't work."

"Try to escape?" Arnold spoke slowly and wrinkled his forehead.

"You're not getting out of here. The building is surrounded. Do you want to die today, Arnold?"

"Ken here's been keeping me alive since that night at Tipper's Point." Arnold smiled. "Tell him, Ken."

Ken shook his head and Arnold readjusted himself against him.

"What's he talking about Ken? What did you do?" Noah asked.

"Your boy here wanted to work with me. He not only wanted to help me get away with it. He wanted to help me kill."

"Shut up." Ken yelled.

"He knows now, Ken. You know what you have to do." Beads of sweat drip down Arnold's forehead.

Noah thought he saw Ken's eyes flicker and he aimed his gun at Arnold.

"Cotter knows you've been helping me. I knew you'd caught on, Cotter. I just didn't know how much you knew. That's why I chose you." Arnold said. "How else could I have known the police were coming to Tipper's Point? How else could I have known the location of the safe house? Your cop lady though—now Ken, you didn't have my back for that. You were supposed to tell me about security at the park, but you didn't tell me that black cop would be there."

Noah watched Ken's face, and in the moments Arnold spoke, he knew the words were true.

"You didn't have to tell him," Ken looked back at Arnold, "why did you tell him?"

Arnold let go of Ken, pulled the gun from his head, and put it in his hand. He stayed behind him, as Ken raised his gun, and Arnold used the door handle to prop himself up.

"I couldn't have gotten away on my own." Arnold leaned in toward his ear. "Think about it Ken, just kill him and say I did it. We can keep working together, you and I. We can finish this together."

"Ken, shoot him!" Noah yelled and Arnold opened the door, which set off an alarm.

"I'll see you soon Ken. You know how to get in touch." Arnold slipped out the door.

Noah started after him, but Ken kept the gun aimed at Noah.

"Awh, Ken. He's getting away. You didn't... you didn't do anything. We can still fix this."

"Don't play stupid." Ken shook his head.

"He can't get away."

The ringing intensified everything and Noah knew he had to make a move.

"I'm sorry, Noah. I really am."

Ken pushed his finger against the trigger and a bang echoed in the alcove.

Chapter 42

THE SHOT RANG IN NOAH'S ears and he felt someone grab him from behind. Ken clutched at his arm, slumped against the wall across from him.

"Noah, what happened?" Ethan hollered at him.

Ken moaned and squeezed his eyes shut.

"Ken's been working for Arnold. He was going to shoot me. He let Arnold get away." Noah struggled out of Ethan's grasp as the door slammed the wall and Palfry stood in the frame. "He's getting away!"

Ethan nodded to Palfry, and he slipped back inside the building.

Noah ran past Ken to the door.

"Noah, stop!"

"He's getting away Ethan!"

"Palfry's getting security after him. Who shot Ken?"

"I did. He was working with Arnold. They both admitted it!" Noah opened the door and looked outside.

The walkway was empty until the parking lot, where a nurse stood smoking.

A nurse came through the door, and another rushed in after her toward Ken.

"He's dangerous!" Noah shouted. "You have to cuff him."

Noah started out the door, but Ethan grabbed his arm. "I can't let you go right now, Noah."

"You don't believe me? You don't believe Ken was helping him? That he was going to shoot me?"

"I can't let you go."

Palfry panted as he entered the alcove. "Security's after him now. Cotter, what the hell happened?"

"Ask him." Noah nodded toward Ken.

"Ken? Ken is it true?" Ethan knelt down beside him, as another nurse came in with a bed.

"Oh God." Ken squirmed.

"Ken!" Ethan yelled, but the nurses pushed him away as they helped him onto the bed.

Noah opened the door, and hung in the opening, watching Palfry.

Palfry nodded, and Noah was out the door before Ethan could say go.

Noah looked both ways and ran to the parking lot. He saw nothing unusual, and ran down to the sidewalk into the underground parking lot.

Engines hummed, and the laughter of two women echoed throughout.

Noah checked the ground around the entry, but there was no sign of blood. Only oil stains.

"Security!" He heard a deep voice call, and ran toward it with his gun drawn.

A security officer jogged toward a man in a suit with blood on his forehead.

"Some asshole punched me and stole my car!" The man hollered.

"In a hospital gown?" Noah asked, and the man nodded. "How long ago?"

"This just happened."

"Did he drive out of here?"

The man nodded and rubbed his head.

Noah got the car make and license plate, and ran back to the building.

He called the license plate in over the radio on his way back to the alcove.

Ethan and Palfry followed Ken into a room, and Noah ran after them and pulled Ethan out.

"He stole a man's car. I've got the license plate. We need--"

"How did he get past security?" Palfry came out of the room and put his hands on his hips. "He does not get away. I want eyes in the sky and--"

"I'm going after him."

Ethan nodded and took his keys out of his pocket.

Noah grabbed them and as he ran down the hallway, Ethan called to him.

"P2, by the elevator!"

Noah ran out the front doors, and on his way to the car, he called January.

"Tell me they're safe."

"Yes, they're fine. They're with me. What happened?"

"It was Ken. Ken was working with Arnold."

"Bastard!"

"I shot him. Arnold got away. I'm going after him."

"Okay, I'll take care of them."

"Thanks."

"Catch him, Noah."

Chapter 43

"I CAN'T BELIEVE IT." January pressed a button on her phone and slipped it into her pocket. "I can't believe this."

"January?" Charla whispered.

"Arnold was working with someone on our team. With our tech analyst. He helped him escape."

"Arnold's gone?" Charla asked, and as the words seeped into Avery's thoughts she sat down on the floor.

He's gone. Free.

"Avery?" January walked over to her. "Cotter's going after him."

She started to shake, and Charla took Louie's leash before she kneeled down beside her.

"How?" Charla asked. "How did they do it?"

"I don't know, but Ken helped him somehow." January rubbed Avery's back.

"I ran him over." Avery screamed, and rocked back and forth. "I hit him hard. How is he--"

"You did, and it will make it easier to catch him." January stood and gave her room, "He's not here. You're safe."

Avery shook her head. "No."

"It was a distraction." Charla leaned against the door frame. "He didn't want to see me. He used me."

"You can't trust anything he says, Charla. That's what we were trying to tell you. He's sick. You can't begin to understand him, or reason with him."

Charla shook her head and crossed her arms.

"He's not the man you thought you knew, and I know that's hard to accept, and it will take time." January pulled Charla in for a hug." We have to go back now. We have to let them know you're both okay."

January reach down to Avery and pulled her up. "What are we going to do?"

"We are going home, girls." January rested her hand on Avery's back and led her out of the room.

Avery wiped tears from her eyes and wrapped her arms over her stomach as January led them into the hallway. Charla passed Louie's leash back to Avery, and rested her hand over hers for a moment.

Louie followed them to the stair case, and led them back up the stairs to the fourth floor.

"January!" Ethan called.

With a girl in each arm, January walked over to him.

"I'm taking these girls home when Noah gets back. They need to go back."

"Can I have a word alone with you?"

January let her arms fall from their shoulders. "Could you wait over there girls? Right there?"

They nodded and she walked a few feet away with Ethan.

"What good is going home if Arnold will be there waiting for us?" Avery asked.

"Maybe they already caught him." Charla said.

As they stood in the silence that followed, Avery was sure neither believed the words she spoke.

Chapter 44

THE MOMENT THE CALL from the helicopter came in, Noah turned the car around and headed south toward the highway.

He had taken a chance on Arnold fleeing north, to isolated areas, and places he was familiar with.

Noah stopped before Bloor Street and turned left. He followed the road toward the area helicopter hovered over.

A rest stop with fast food chains in one building.

Noah arrived moments before two police cruisers and ran to the car.

Empty.

Blood stained the driver's seat, but otherwise, the car was clean.

"You, search the building. You, cover the back exit." Noah shouted over the hum of the chopper over head.

The officers ran toward the building, while Noah looked across the road, and scanned the sidewalks.

"Did anyone see a man get out of this car?" He hollered into the parking lot.

A couple passing by shook their heads, and a man leaving with a coffee didn't even look his way.

He scanned the cars for anyone who might have been sitting in their vehicles, but the few parked were empty.

An officer ran toward him.

"Clear. He's not in there. Not in the restrooms. Nothing."

Noah heard his cell phone ring, and saw Palfry's name on the I.D.

"Cotter." He covered his other ear with his finger.

"The pilot says the car was abandoned when he got there."

"He's not in the building." Noah hollered back.

"The chopper's going to search that area. They have your number if they find anything."

Noah hung up and pointed up.

"Get your guys to drive around this area. He's wearing a hospital gown, but he could have changed by now. Have them ask around."

The officer nodded and ran back to the building where another officer emerged shaking his head.

Noah thought about searching the area, but if Arnold stole someone's vehicle from the lot, he wanted to be there when they reported it.

He could have hitch hiked, but who would pick up a bloody man in a hospital gown?

Noah looked across the parking lot, and saw a big rig heading toward the exit.

He got in his car and flicked the sirens on.

The truck slowed down, and Noah swerved his car to a stop in front of it.

"I have to check your load." He hollered, and the driver opened his door and hopped down.

"What's this about?"

"We have a suspect who fled to this area." Noah showed him his badge and ran to the back. He pulled out his gun.

The trucker followed. "I keep it locked."

"Open it." Noah said.

"It's empty." He pulled out his key, and turned it in the lock. "On my way back from a delivery."

"Open it."

The trucker yanked the doors open and Noah took aim.

Empty.

"Told you." He put his hands on his hips. "I gotta go buddy, I'm late."

"Yeah, fine." Noah waved him off and walked back to his car.

How did you get away, Arnold, and where are you going?

Chapter 45

Noah stormed down the hallway. "Where is he?"

"He just finished in surgery." Ethan said. "We're going to sort this out."

Noah continued toward the door to Ken's room, and Ethan pulled him back.

"He lied to us," Noah yelled.

"Keep your voice down, Cotter." Palfry hollered with the same volume.

"We waited for you to speak with him." Ethan said.

Noah saw January sitting with the girls in the nearby waiting room and his eyes met with Avery's.

The lump in his throat made it hard to swallow, and he looked back at Ethan.

"I'm ready. Let's go."

Noah followed them into Ken's room.

He sat propped up in his bed, with a bag of morphine to this left.

"I can help you." Ken looked at Ethan and then to Noah. "I wouldn't have shot you."

"Shut up, Ken. You don't talk unless you're spoken to." Ethan dragged a chair across the floor to sit beside him.

"I'm sorry boss. I really— "

"You tell me everything that happened. You tell me the whole story, and if I find out you lied to me, even once, I'll see you get the maximum for this." Ethan sneered at him. "Start talking."

Ken sucked air through his nose, and his chest heaved up and down.

"I spoke to Owen on the phone when he was at Jennifer Hornby's the day Arnold came in. That first day you both questioned him. When Owen was searching for evidence, he sounded funny. Irritated."

Noah remembered his conversation with his friend, and the heated words they exchanged when they were waiting on Owen to find some hard evidence to use. He thought it had been the pressure to keep Arnold behind bars, but he admitted to being contacted by Bob Pope at that time and being blackmailed into taking Avery and Fiona to Arnold.

Hindsight.

"I traced the last numbers he called on his phone, but there wasn't anything unusual. I looked at the cell phone activity at Jennifer Hornby's and picked up a signal. I traced the number."

"Why didn't you come to me with this? If you were concerned for Owen?"

"I don't know. I didn't want to bother you if it wasn't anything to be worried about. I don't know." Ken looked down at his arm in the sling. "I called the number."

"And it was Arnold." Noah said.

"No, no one answered, but I had a feeling. Like I said, no proof though. I traced Owen's cell phone back to Fiona's. Then to Avery's friend's place. Sadie's. He had two different phones with him."

"You knew something was going on, and you didn't tell me." Ethan's voice shook.

"Outside Avery's friend's place, Owen got another call from the number. I still didn't know for sure..."

"Save it." Ethan looked back at Palfry.

"I traced it to Tipper's Point. I knew that's where you were headed, so I called again. Nothing. I swear, at that point, I was going to tell you, but I couldn't get a hold of you, or anyone. While you were all there, at Tipper's Point, I traced the cells and it looked like Owen was headed back to Birch Falls."

"Owen dumped it in the park garbage there." Noah muttered.

Ken nodded. "I went there, I found it, and I called the only number in the phone. Arnold picked up."

"Be honest with me, Ken. We're getting to the part where you want to make sure you tell me everything." Ken took a deep breath as Ethan spoke the cold and calculated words.

"I told him I knew he was at Tipper's Point with the girls. I knew that Owen brought them there."

"Shit." Palfry said.

"He said thanks and hung up. I knew I screwed up," Ken looked up at Ethan, "I knew I screwed up bad. He called me after, when you were all in the hospital, and told me he had a deal for me. He said if I helped him, he wouldn't kill my parents. He told me it could be a secret, between us."

Ethan stood from the chair, and Noah pulled him back.

"Ethan." Palfry shouted.

He stopped fighting and let Noah pull him back.

"You helped him!" Ethan shook.

"He black-mailed me!"

"No, this goes way beyond." Ethan couldn't form the words and walked back toward the door. "Just tell us what happened."

"He asked me where Darrel Beelson was, and I tracked him down. He asked me to let him know where the police detail was and I did it. He asked me where the safe house was, and I told him I wasn't doing this for him anymore. I told him no. He sent me a video from his phone of my parents eating dinner. He was there, outside their window. He knew where they were."

"Go on." Palfry said.

"He told me it was the last thing he'd ask of me, and that he'd leave me and my family alone if I told him."

"Coward." Ethan spat.

"When I heard that he got caught, I was relieved, and then..."

"Then you got scared that he'd tell us you helped him." Noah said. "So you volunteered to plant the camera in his room to see him. So you could help him escape?"

Ken looked up at Noah. "I wanted to stop him for good. I needed a way to get in and make sure he couldn't tell the truth, but he was ready, he knew I'd come. Put the gun on me to get out. He told you before I could."

"You're finished." Ethan pointed at him and strode out of the room.

"You don't even know what you've done, do you?" Noah asked, and Ken looked up at him.

Noah cuffed Ken to the bed, and turned to leave with Palfry.

"I'm sorry." Ken yelled. "He tricked me too. He used me like he used Owen."

When they got down the hall, Ethan approached them, and shoved his hands in his pockets.

"This is how it'll go," Palfry looked at Ethan, "we'll bring him back with us. Cotter, you and January take the girls back. We'll meet you there. I want to know everything Ken knows and I want those girls safe."

Noah nodded.

"I know this falls on me." Ethan said. "First Owen, now Ken. I'm responsible for them. This is my team. This is my fault."

Palfry looked at Ethan. "I'll assign you a new tech specialist."

"Sir?" Ethan asked.

"Was there something I said you don't understand?" Palfry asked.

Ethan shook his head.

"We have to catch this guy, and I need my best inspector on the case." Palfry turned back to Ken's room.

"Ethan?" Noah asked, and he shook out of his daze. "I'm going to let Ralph know what's going on before we leave."

Ethan nodded. "I don't know how it got past me."

"Arnold uses people to get to the people he really wants. We know this, we can stay ahead of him this way."

"If you get Arnold in your sights again," Ethan turned to him, "you make sure he can't get away."

Noah pressed his lips together and stared back at him.

He knew exactly what he meant.

Chapter 46

LOUIE PAWED AT THE WINDOW and it reminded Avery of the moments after she hit Arnold.

"Can you roll the window down please?" Avery asked. "Just a bit for Louie."

Noah rolled it down. "That okay back there?"

Louie hopped up on Avery's lap and stretched to put his nose out the small opening. The breeze blew through her hair and Avery nodded. Her eyes met his in the rear view mirror.

His stare seemed blank, and Avery broke their gaze when she noticed January watching them.

Charla rested her head against her window, and ignored Louie when he approached her for snuggles.

"You'll both have to stay with us for a while." Noah said.

"What about Louie?" Avery asked.

"You might need to drop him off at Sadie's for the time being."

Avery nodded. "The police station's no place for a dog anyway. The hospital was bad enough. Sadie or Josh will take him for a while."

She flipped her cell phone open and sent Sadie a message.

Mind if Louie stays with you for a while? If you'd rather not, I can ask Josh.

For the time they were apart, she had wished Noah could be with her.

Be there for her.

As they sat in the same car with failure and desperation in the air, she wondered if she had imagine their connection during their time apart.

Made it into something it never was.

Never would be.

Never should be with everything that had happened.

Of course Louie can stay with me. When will you be back?

On our way now.

January put her phone to her ear. "On route now. All clear."

Avery caught Noah watching her again, switching his focus from the road back to her every few seconds.

She wondered if he was trying to tell her something.

"We'll be stopping off at Avery's friend's place. Sadie's. Yeah, the dog."

BARE YOUR BONES

Noah ran his fingers through his hair and leaned toward the open window. He rested his head on his hand, and glanced back at her over his left shoulder.

It was only a second, but she felt the connection again.

They were close enough to touch, and yet they couldn't.

Maybe it's better this way, she thought, better for everyone.

⤴

The emptiness Charla felt grew deeper as they crossed the city line into Birch Falls.

Before she met Avery at the cafe, she truly believed that getting the lie off her shoulders that she had held for so long would release her from her guilt.

She kept playing the moments after their meeting in her mind as her last normal moments.

Charla looked over at Avery and wondered if she felt the same.

Rain fell onto the windows and she felt drips on her arms before Inspector Cotter rolled his window up.

The tiny taps on the window turned into splatters and Charla found herself mesmerized by them.

Drops ran into others, and became bigger as they slid across the window, until the car slowed to a stop.

"I'll be right back." Avery said as they parked in the driveway.

Charla watched Sadie open her door and squint out at them through the rain.

When Avery stepped inside the door, although it was dark, Charla made out their figures clearly.

They hugged and the embrace lasted almost a minute.

Charla's chest felt heavy, and she wished she had someone to hug her. Someone who'd known her for so long.

Someone who loved her.

Tears slid down her cheeks and she wiped them away.

She thought she saw January look away from her, but she couldn't tell for sure, and when Inspector Cotter opened the door again, Charla crossed her arms tight to her chest.

Avery dropped into her seat, and the door shut.

The damp air sat in the car with them as they pulled out of the driveway and Charla's head started to ache.

I had that relationship.

I had that love.

And he took it from me.

For the first time, her need to find the reason why was overshadowed by her need to feel loved.

I'll never feel that love again.

As she watched the drops of water find each other on the window, she lost herself in a flood of tears.

Chapter 47

"YOU'RE GOING TO TELL us everything you know about Arnold." Ethan leaned in and rested his arms on the table

"Why would he tell us?" Noah scowled at Ken, "Are you still working for him? Is this part of the plan?"

Ken looked back to Ethan. "I'll tell you because I want to see that bastard go down for all this like he should have before. I don't want him to threaten my family, or anyone else's ever again."

"You don't believe him, do you?"

Ethan studied Ken. "I believe you."

Noah shook his head and pushed his chair out from the table. January stepped into the room, and sat on the other side of Ethan before she slipped a folder in front of him. Noah sat back down and rubbed the stubble on his chin.

Ethan set his hand on the folder. "You have the right to a lawyer."

"I waive my right," Ken looked to Noah, "if you don't believe me now, you never will."

Ethan slid the folder across the table without looking at it.

Ken opened it, read the front page, and flipped to the last. He looked up at Ethan and nodded.

January handed Ethan a pen, and he pushed it across the table to Ken. He signed each page, and set the pen on the folder when he was done.

"I can't take this. How can you give him a deal when you don't even know if he knows anything relevant?" Noah shook his head and looked at the ceiling. "How can you believe him?"

"If you remember, Noah, I told Ken what would happen if I found out he told me one lie. That's why I have to explore this further."

January pushed her chair back and crossed her arms.

"You better start talking." Ethan said.

"Are Charla and Avery here? Safe?" Ken asked.

"You'll never have a right to know their whereabouts." Noah said.

"I'll assume you've got them somewhere safe." Ken said, and looked to Ethan, "Next, I'd suggest Sadie and Josh."

"He knows about them?" Noah raised his voice."You told him?"

Ken shook his head. "He told me. He used it as part of his threat."

Ethan nodded to January, and her black heels clipped along out of the room.

"Does he know who Charla really is?" Noah asked.

"No, I never told him that. He never really asked about her." Ken shrugged.

"Where is he?" Ethan asked.

"I don't know for sure— "

"Liar." Noah muttered under his breath.

"Noah, do you need to leave too?" Ethan asked. "Ken, where is he?"

"He never told me where he was, but I traced his cell phone, and it stopped at the Crown River Produce most nights."

"So you knew where he was?" Ethan asked.

"I drove by one night. I thought if I saw him there, I could go back and..." Ken looked down at the table. "I thought I could finish it all myself. But he wasn't there, and the parking lot was so crowded. I lost my nerve."

"Where would he be then?" Ethan asked.

"I did some digging, and there's a subdivision nearby. Housing for abused men and their families."

"Are you— " Noah felt the anger flow within, and he could have appreciated the irony if it were another situation, but he fought the urge to jump across the table and strangle Ken himself.

"I know which houses, and I know who the owner is. It's not for sure, but it's all I could come up with, and he's twisted enough that he just might pretend to be an abused man."

"You don't get to judge him." Noah scoffed.

"What are you waiting for?" Ethan asked. "Give us the address."

⁓

"I've been thinking, maybe I should move away." Charla picked a chip out of the bag, and tossed it back in again.

"How far?" Avery sat down at the table across from her.

"Maybe the States? Maybe Australia. I've always thought about traveling to the Gold Coast."

"Have you ever thought about living there?"

Charla shook her head. "I always thought I'd be here. Make a family near mine."

"Yeah." Avery rested her head on her hand. "Somewhere far might be best."

"January said she'd help me find a new home, set myself up, but I think they want to wait until they catch him. I can't wait that long."

"I know what you mean." Avery checked her cell phone as it rang.

Parents. She pressed ignore.

"I'm going nuts worrying about everything. If I was away, maybe I could— " Charla searched the room with her eyes, "breathe."

The cramped office was a poor excuse for a place to stay, but Avery felt safe there among the stacks of files.

Charla felt trapped.

Avery picked a chip from the bag. "I'm sure January will help you, if that's what you want."

"Yeah, she's been awesome. I thought I'd stay, but I don't have any real ties here. There's nothing keeping me here. No part of me that wants to stay anymore. Is it wrong to want to run away?"

A tap at the door made Charla jump, and January popped her head inside.

"You girls alright?"

They nodded.

"I've got something for you Avery." She smiled.

"Hmm?" Avery watched January step back from the door, and Sadie rushed into the room.

"Avery!"

"Sadie." Avery stood up and Sadie wrapped her arms around her neck.

Sadie let her go and when she stepped away, her smile faded.

"What?" Avery asked.

Sadie glanced at Charla and back to Avery. "Arnold knows about me and where I live."

"What?" Charla asked. "How?"

"Ken, the man who was working with us. He told us." January leaned her back against the door. "I told your friend, Josh, and he told me he wasn't able to come in. He said he had to work."

Avery looked to Sadie, "Why?"

"He told me I should come in, but that he didn't want to live that way."

"He appreciated the warning," January said, "and we've got a car outside his home watching anyway. Same with Sadie's. I've got to go out for a while, but I'll be back shortly, and I'll get you a proper dinner. No more vending machine food."

"Thanks." Avery pulled her chair out and sat down again.

"January?" Charla said. "Can I talk to you when you get back?"

January nodded and left the room.

"I'm worried about Josh." Sadie sat down to the table. "I think he *wants* to meet Arnold."

"What do you mean?" Charla asked.

"I think his anger and frustration with the whole thing has come to a boiling point." Sadie shrugged. "He told me he's not afraid."

"He needs to be." Charla said. "Does he not know what Arnold has done?"

Sadie looked down at the table.

"Josh needs to come in." Avery said. "Arnold killed Red and Blue. They were trained to protect us. I don't know what I'd do if something happened to him. And Asher, and Jack."

"Then you need to talk to him, because I couldn't argue. He's at the shelter now."

"I'll ask him to come in to see me. He'll do that. Maybe we can get him to stay."

Sadie raised her brows and stared at Avery.

"I'm sorry I brought you into this. Before we left, we were assured you and Josh would be safe. That Arnold didn't know about you. How could he have known?"

"He could have been following you." Charla said. "He could have gotten the information from their guy. He always gets what he wants."

"That's why I need Josh to take this seriously." Avery said.

"Oh he does," Sadie pursed her lips, "Josh bought a gun when you were in the hospital the first time. Now, he just wants an excuse to use it."

Charla shook her head with tears in her eyes. "Red and Blue had guns. It won't matter."

"He's not invincible." Sadie said.

"No," Avery muttered, "but nothing's stopped him yet."

"He's a monster." Charla whispered and a few tears fell from her eyes.

Sadie rummaged through her purse, and offered Charla a tissue. She took it and shook her head.

"If you care at all about his life," Charla looked down at the tissue, "you need to get him in here."

"I'm calling Josh now."

Chapter 48

Noah peered through his window at the last townhouse on Chicamata Drive. They got there before the sun set, and there had been no activity on the street since.

"January, is everyone in place?" Noah spoke into his radio.

"Ready." January's voice crackled back a moment later.

Ethan nodded and dialed Palfry's number.

"We're here and there's no sign of him."

"Owner of the properties said he only met him twice, and that his facial hair made him unrecognizable. Said he was getting out of a bad situation."

Ethan and Noah exchanged glances. "I'd like to wait and see if he shows."

"No," Palfry's voice consumed the frequency, "we don't wait on him anymore. He could be in there. He could have his next victim already."

"I understand." Ethan rubbed his forehead, " I don't want to lose him either."

"Again." Palfry quipped.

"Yes, but I think we are missing a real opportunity here."

"Is the team ready?"

"Yes, but— "

"Now." Palfry's voice boomed.

"We're going in." Ethan said and nodded to Noah.

"January, we're going in."

"Now?"

"Now."

Ethan and Noah got out of the car, and Noah grabbed his gun from the holster.

If you're here, you're not getting away again.

He and Ethan climbed the stairs to the small shared porch. He remembered what Ethan told him.

No matter what.

Ethan looked at him, gun drawn, and nodded twice. He signaled for two officers to go around the back, and as he kicked the door down, Noah saw January drive up to the townhouse.

Ethan went in first and Noah followed. He went into the living room, and Noah continued down the hall. It was small, without any decorations. Nothing personal hung on the walls or sitting on the tables.

"Clear." Ethan yelled.

As Noah passed the stairs, he smelled something bad.

Something rotting.

He reached the kitchen.

"Clear."

Noah opened the back door for two officers.

"Nothing back here." The black woman said.

Noah nodded, and went back to the front door, as Ethan climbed the stairs.

The smell got stronger, and after Ethan cleared the bathroom, Noah hesitated in front of the master bedroom, where the door was slightly ajar.

The smell was distinct, and when he felt Ethan behind him, he opened it all the way.

A young woman's bloody body laid on the floor, and brown marks stained the taupe carpet of the entire room.

"We've got a body!" Ethan called, and an officer hollered back.

Noah heard someone coming up the stairs, but he couldn't take his eyes off the mirror above the dresser.

TOO LATE was written across the wall in blood.

"He's taunting us. Trying to make you lose focus, Noah." Ethan said, and January stepped beside him. "He's not here."

"From the looks of things, he wasn't coming back." January said and walked over to the body.

Noah and Ethan stood at the woman's feet, and stared at her t-shirt. Dry blood coated her stomach, and it reminded Noah of Avery.

January put on gloves, and pulled her shirt up.

Three deep slashes across her stomach, one revealing her pelvic bone.

"This looks like Avery's... sort of." January whispered.

"I think he meant it to." Noah stepped back from the body.

"She wasn't tied up," Ethan said, "and it looks like this could have happened before he found the safe house."

"Do you think there is significance to the number of cuts? Like Avery's?" January asked.

Noah said and ran his fingers through his hair. "He sliced through Lisa Carson once, Lilith Temple twice, and this girl three times."

"And Avery ten." Ethan added.

"He's counting down to her." Noah said.

"Actually," January spoke softly, "he's counting up."

"He wants her to be his tenth." Noah glanced down at the body. "He's already marked her for that."

As he said the words sunk in he wanted to leave. He wanted to go to Avery.

January shook her head. "Why did he go to the safe house then? By your theory, he wouldn't have killed her."

"Maybe he just wanted to kill Charla?" Ethan said.

"He's torturing Avery. Making her suffer." Noah looked down at the body. "He's saving her for last."

⤴

Josh walked into the room and Avery and Sadie both ran into his arms.

"Hey," he pulled away and looked at Avery, "I'm glad you're okay."

Avery smiled at him, and looked back at Charla. "This is Charla. Charla, this is my other best friend, Josh."

"I'm not staying, but I wanted to come and see you."

"Josh," Sadie squeezed his arm, "I don't think you understand."

"I understand this is serious, trust me, I get that."

Avery went back to her chair and stood behind it.

"I don't want to do this Josh," she propped herself up by the back of the chair, "but will you do it for me? For Sadie and me?"

"I will consider coming back to see you, alright? I have to make sure Asher is safe. I don't want to leave him."

"I get that," Sadie said, "but if it's about him, bring him in too."

He shook his head. "He says if I come here, he's moving out."

"Maybe that's for the best," Charla said, and they all turned to her.

"I'm sorry?" Josh said.

"I don't know you, or Asher, I don't know anyone here very well. I don't even know Arnold anymore, but I do know that if you make the mistake of thinking you can go against him, you'll pay with your life. Or your loved ones."

Josh cleared his throat. "You're right. You don't know me. I'm not going to run from this psycho. I'm not letting him get in my head, or hurt my boyfriend."

Charla opened her mouth, but Josh went on.

"You girls are safe here, and I'll keep Asher and I safe."

"Josh," Sadie said, but he raised his hand.

"I've gotta get going." He went to open the door, and Avery rushed up behind him and grabbed his hand.

"If anything happens to you," she whispered, "I don't think I could live with myself."

The door opened and hit Josh, pushing him out of the way.

"Whoa, sorry." Noah closed the door behind him. "I'm glad you're both here."

"I was actually just leaving." Josh said.

"Are you sure?" Noah asked.

"Tell him, Noah, please." Avery whimpered. "Tell him he shouldn't leave."

Noah looked at Josh, and his puffed out chest lifted up and down.

"Arnold knows where you and Sadie live. He'll be watching for you and trying to use you against Avery.

I get that you don't want to stay here, but you need to understand the risk you're taking."

Josh nodded. "I'll take that into consideration. I'm glad you've got Sadie and Avery here."

"I won't let anything happen to them."

Josh nodded and slipped out the door.

"You say that," Charla said, "but we've been told that before. My family was told the same thing."

"I am doing everything I can." Noah said.

"It's not enough. It's never going to be enough." Charla stood. "Is January back yet?"

"She'll be in shortly. I don't want you to be afraid." Noah said. "I know that's difficult right now, but while you're with us, you're safe."

Sadie nodded, and sat down at the table with Charla.

Noah looked at Avery, and she stared back at him. "While you're with me, you're safe."

Avery lost herself in his eyes, and everything in the room seemed to fade.

"I want to believe that." She whispered.

"I won't let anything happen to you." His voice was clear and steady.

A knock on the door drew their attention and January stepped in.

"Hey Charla, can I talk to you for a bit?"

Charla hurried across the room, and closed the door behind them.

"Is there any news?" Avery asked.

"Let's sit down, okay?"

Avery nodded and tucked her hair behind her ear before she sat.

"We found the place where Arnold was hiding while he was here. We also found another body."

"Do you know her? Do I know her?" Avery asked.

"No, she's not connected in any way that I know of."

"How?" Avery asked.

"I don't want to get into the details. I don't think you really want to know much more than that, do you?"

"I don't want to be in the dark."

Noah rested his hands on his hips. "Josh should really stay here for the time being, but I can't make him."

"That's what we were trying to get him to do." Sadie said.

"Alright, well I just came to check on you. January will be back soon to see if you need anything."

Avery nodded and he stood to leave the room.

"Noah?" Avery called, "Do you think he's still here?"

"I can't say. Just know that I meant what I said. I'm going to protect you."

Chapter 49

CHARLA FOLLOWED JANUARY DOWN a long hallway, past a room with cubicles, and into an office on the left. The brown desk and chair gave the room a warmer vibe than the one they stayed in and January sat down behind the desk.

"Want to settle in?" She asked, and opened the laptop.

Charla sat down and stared up at a large picture of seagulls above the ocean. The waves seemed to twist and turn.

"This is Inspector Cotter's office. He said we could borrow it for a bit. I wanted to talk to you about something I promised you a while ago. Setting up a new life for you."

"Right," Charla pushed the chair in closer to the desk, "I've been thinking about it. I'd like to relocate."

"Okay, where?"

"Another province maybe or country."

"I see. Did you ever have plans before all this to move so far away?"

Charla shook her head. "If I'm going to move, I want it to be as soon as possible. Regardless of whether you catch Arnold now or later. I want to go now."

"I promise I'm going to help you, no matter what your decision is, but I want to make sure you're making the right one for you. Will you humor me for a moment?"

Charla nodded and set her hands in her lap.

"Where in particular would you like me to look?"

"Maybe British Columbia? If not, I was thinking Maine."

"Okay," January pushed away from the laptop, and leaned in on the table, "what if I told you it would take a month to set this up?"

"That's too long. I don't think I could do a month. I'm sick of this. Looking over my shoulder, having family and people I know murdered, by my own father. I don't have a home. I don't have family." Tears welled up in her eyes. "This is going to sound crazy, but you're the closest thing I have to a friend right now. You're the only one who knows what I've been through, who's tried to be there for me."

"You feel alone, but if you leave, you'll truly be alone. Here, like you said, you have me, and Avery."

"No. What makes me feel more alone than anything is watching Avery with her friends. The people who love her and care about her. It's not her fault, but it's in my face all the time, even when her friends aren't here. She seems close with Inspector Cotter too."

"I can't imagine how you're feeling, but I want you to know that I care about you, alright? You're a strong girl, Charla. You're going to be alright."

Charla broke into sobs, and January rounded the desk, and rubbed her back.

"What if nobody ever loves me again?"

"Charla, please don't say that. It's not true, you deserve to be loved, and cared for, and protected."

"Avery has forgiven me for my part in this, " Charla tried to catch her breath, "but I'm his daughter. I'm his flesh and blood. As long as he's alive, I'll always be connected to him."

"You're not your father, Charla."

Charla buried her face in her hands and wept.

January pulled her up and wrapped her arms around her.

"I know," January whispered in her ear, "I know it hurts and I know you're in deep pain. If you want to get out of here, I'll help you. It won't take a month, but it might take a few days. Can you hang in for just a little longer?"

Charla nodded into January's shoulder and she held her tight through her tears.

Noah opened the door to his office and started to shut it again.

"No, it's okay." January rubbed Charla's back. "We're through in here now."

Charla turned around with red eyes and wiped at them.

"You sure?"

Charla nodded.

"Charla, I'll meet you back with Avery and Sadie. I'll bring dinner, alright?"

Charla hung her head as she left.

Noah went behind his desk and opened his laptop. "She alright?"

"No and I didn't expect her to be. I'm glad she opened up to me though. I'm finding a safe place for her."

"Do you think that's a good idea?"

"I understand why she wants to leave, and we can't hold her here, so I'm going to help her."

"What if Arnold follows her? Finds her?"

"You said yourself, it's Avery he's after." January closed the door. "I have to talk to you about her."

"Avery?" Noah looked up from his e-mails.

"What's going on with you and her?"

He looked back down at his computer and opened an email. "What do you mean?"

"You know what I mean. Come on, you know you can talk to me about this."

Noah deleted the email, and went to the next. Lisa Carson's friend, Michelle.

"Do you have feelings for her?" January stepped forward. "Has something happened between you? Something personal?"

Michelle sent him a list of Lisa's past boyfriends. Only two had a last name included, neither of which he recognized.

"Noah."

He looked up at her and sighed. "Yes. I have feelings for her. No, nothing's happened."

"She calls you by your first name, she trusts you. The way she looks at you. I can tell she does. This is bad, Noah. You getting close could—"

"You're close with Charla. You've agreed to send her away without consulting Ethan, or Palfry, or me. You *told* me. You didn't even ask what I think."

"Don't put this on me. Don't change the subject. I believe you when you say nothing has happened, and I trust that you understand nothing can. Not any time soon."

Noah averted her stare and went back to the list.

"I won't say anything to anyone, but if you don't keep things professional, I will."

To a name he recognized.

"January."

"I'm sorry. I don't want to, but this case has been—"

"January. Come look at this. Lisa Carson's friend Michelle got back to me. You told me to check with her friend, and I asked her to send me a list of Lisa's past boyfriends. She sent this to me yesterday."

Noah pointed to the second name on the list. January blinked and looked at him.

"No."

"It makes sense."

"There's no last name. We can't be sure."

"Not yet, " Noah pushed his chair out from the desk, "but I know a way to find out. Don't say anything yet, alright?"

January nodded. "But you'll let me know?"

"As soon as I do."

⤴

Noah entered Room C, and an unfamiliar face stared back at him.

"Hi, I'm Tansy." She smiled up at him from behind the computer screen, which added a warm glow to her light brown skin. "I'm the new Technical Analyst."

"Hi, nice to meet you." Noah reached out his hand, and she shook it softly. "I'm Inspector Noah Cotter."

"I know who you are," she nodded, " and I'm all caught up."

Ethan entered the room with a flash drive in his hand.

"That's it." He handed it to her. "That's everything we have."

Tansy inserted the drive into the laptop, and typed at an unusually fast speed.

"I see you've met Inspector Cotter?"

"Just call me Noah."

She nodded without looking up.

"Good. We're just waiting on January." Ethan sat down to the table.

"Actually, I asked Pete if he'd come in on the case with us in Ralph's role until he's back, pending your approval."

"Alright, I'll trust you on that. We need some manpower behind us anyway. Good."

The door opened and Pete held it for January.

"Pete's going to be working for the team, and Tansy's our new tech." Ethan walked to the dry erase board. "I'd love for us all to get to know each other, but we don't have any time. If you don't know the case, get to know it. Today."

"Charla wants to relocate." January said and sat down.

"Now?" Ethan asked.

"Yes, and if you're concerned, I understand, but I think it's best for everyone if she were relocated. Arnold wouldn't be able to use her, and she would get a chance at a new life. Most importantly, she wouldn't be in danger if only one person knows where she's going."

"You?"

"Yes."

"Okay, good. Work with Tansy on that. Set her up with a flight and then you work alone from there January." Ethan grabbed the marker. "While Noah was briefly the head of this team, I'm back from medical leave in an official capacity, and as the lead inspector. January, I need you with Charla until we relocate her, and then when we decide what to do with Avery and Sadie, you'll be working with Noah. Pete, you're with me until we need you on the streets. You'll be in and out."

"Yes sir,"

Ethan started to draw on the map. "This is Arnold's last known location by Highway 401 in Toronto. This was the last known residence, and the crime scene where the most recent victim was found."

"He left a message at that scene, and everything we've dealt with suggests Arnold believes this is a game." Noah turned his chair back to the table. "He's likely still here, and we've determined his end game is Avery. Each girl he kills is marked by a number of cuts. We believe these cuts represent the count down to Avery."

"Who is the message for?" Pete asked. "Us or Avery?"

"Maybe both but we haven't told her. She doesn't need to know." Ethan stood behind his chair. "He won't be moving around easily. Crown River and the surrounding regions are all on the look out for him. He'll kill again and it will be his fourth marked girl."

"I've been checking the security tapes of businesses in Crown River and Birch Falls, and I haven't found any activity. Unless he picked a spot and hasn't moved, he's likely on the outskirts of town or in Cedar Ridge." Tansy said. "I'll keep checking, but it's a lot of footage to go through, so it would help if the areas could be narrowed down."

"I want security cameras in Crown River Park and Birch Falls Park." Ethan said. "Tansy, I need you to monitor them, and Pete, I want them installed before sun down. If he goes to either of those parks again, I want to see him before he even goes in. We need to make the security around Avery top priority, and Charla is just as important. January and Noah, you stay on those girls. We need a tip. We need someone to call this in." Ethan shook his head. "Or we won't find him until he kills again."

Chapter 50

AFTER SPEAKING WITH LILITH TEMPLE'S mom, Noah discovered she had been single for more than a year.

Her mom couldn't give any names of the men in her life because there were none to give. When she told him she had Lilith's personal possessions from her office delivered to her, Noah asked if he could pick them up.

With the banker's box in his trunk, Noah raced back to his office to scour through it.

Lotion, pens, and pencils.

He pulled a file folder from underneath and opened it.

Empty.

He picked up her badge and studied it.

Maybe Arnold picked her out of convenience, because she was a female cop that left the department at the right time.

A protein bar and a hair tie.

He wondered where her purse was and remembered seeing her in the video. She wasn't wearing one.

He raced through the halls to her old cubicle. Her desk was empty. He opened the drawers, but there was nothing but a protein bar wrapper inside.

"Inspector?" A black cop he recognized stood from her desk. "Are you looking for something?"

"You were at the town house, looking for Arnold Henderson?"

She nodded. "Lilith and I were friends."

"Was she seeing anybody?"

"No."

"Was anything different about her that day or the week she died?"

"Different how? She didn't know Arnold Henderson."

"Is there anything important I should know, I'm sorry, I didn't catch your name."

"Jules." She looked up at him and down at the floor. "She told me something a few days before she died. Something in confidence."

"You have to help me, Jules. I need to know."

"It's not about Arnold Henderson. It was about work."

"Whatever it was, it might be important."

"Lil came to me because I've been here longer than her, and she asked me for advice. She told me a co-worker sexually assaulted her."

"Who?"

"She wouldn't say. She said he grabbed her ass and asked me if I thought she should say something, or if it would make it worse. She said he's someone important here. Someone who's been here a while. She wondered if anyone would believe her. If she should bother filing a report.'"

"What did you say?"

"I told her to tell Terry in HR. I told her that's not something we allow or accept."

"Did she say anything else? Did she say she'd talk to Terry?"

Jules shook her head. "She just thanked me for listening."

"When did this happen?"

"Two days before she was murdered. Or no, it was the day before."

His phone rang, and he held his finger up.

"Cotter, it's Pete."

"Do you have something?"

"Yeah, the latest victim from the town house was identified. Her name's Georgia Watson."

"Thanks Pete, how did you find out?"

"The news."

"Great. Make sure Ethan knows, alright?"

"Thanks for putting me on the case, I owe ya one, Cotter."

"Can you do me a favor now?"

"Sure."

"Get everyone in Room C. Ethan, January, Tansy, and Ken."

"Ken?"

"I don't have time to explain, but it's important everyone be there."

Noah hung up. "Thank you, Jules."

She nodded. "Catch that cop-killing bastard."

Chapter 51

AVERY WOKE TO THE SOUND of a phone ringing, and as she struggled to climb over Sadie on the air mattress, she realized it came from the office beside them.

Charla was curled up on the couch, and Sadie laid on her back like sleeping beauty. Avery changed and as she headed for the door, her cell phone rang.

"Hey Josh, how are you?" She stepped outside the room and closed the door gently.

"Been better," he sighed, "I've been worried about you and Sadie. What if they don't catch Arnold anytime soon? They'll take you to another safe house."

"I don't know what the plan is Josh, but as long as we are here, you don't have to worry about us. We're worried about you. Have you thought about coming in? Staying with us?"

"I did. I thought about it and talked to Asher about it."

"What did he say?"

"We broke up."

"What? No."

"It's not your fault, or anyone's. It was mutual. He didn't want to be in this situation. I don't blame him. I'm not in the right frame of mind to enjoy a quiet evening at home with him, and the whole thing wasn't fair."

"I'm sorry."

"I was thinking. What if you, Sadie, and I moved away? With Jack and Louie."

A smile crept onto her lips. "You know I would love that, but I can't ask you to do that for me."

"I'd be doing it for all of us. We'd get to be together, some place that's actually safe. No one has to know where we are, and you can start over."

"Josh, I don't know. We wouldn't be doing this if nothing bad had happened. We all have work, and commitments, and Sadie has her family."

"You said it though Avery. We're family."

"We are, but you'd both be giving up too much."

"It's worth it if we'd be safe. Sadie can be a registered massage therapist anywhere. You'll find another teaching job, or do free-lance photography, and we can find another animal shelter to work with. Think about it."

"I'll think about it." Avery smiled.

It sounded good.

Too good.

"Good." She heard a smile in his voice. "I'll talk to Inspector Cotter if you want, or whoever. Talk to Sadie about it too, okay?"

"I will. Thanks Josh. You're too sweet to me."

"Call me later, and let me know."

"I will."

⌒

Noah opened the door to Room C and all eyes were on him.

Ethan stood by the head of the table, and Ken sat to his left with Pete behind him. He set his cuffed hands on the table and gave January, who sat across from him, a dirty look.

"Noah, what's going on?" Ethan asked.

"I heard about the third victim. Georgia Watson." Noah stood beside his usual chair.

"Right," Ethan looked at Ken, "she was Ken's old next-door neighbor."

"I know." Noah sat down and set his paper in front of him. "Ken, do you think Arnold killed her because you knew her? As a threat to keep you quiet about everything?"

Ken nodded. "That's what I thought when I found out."

"What I don't get, is why he'd go after an old neighbor of yours? After you divorced, you moved out. How would Arnold even know where you used to live?""

"My wife lives there still. Noah, you think he'll try to kill my ex-wife?"

"I was sent an email from Lisa Carson's friend, Michelle. She sent me a list of Lisa's past boyfriends.""

Ken and Ethan shared the same confused stare.

"We checked out the list, and guess whose name we found?" January asked.

"I'm not in the mood for games." Ethan crossed his arms.

"Ken." Noah stood.

"What?" Ken looked up at him. "I didn't know her."

"I didn't say you did. I just said we found someone with the same name on that list. Isn't that a coincidence?"

Ken stared up at him.

"I don't understand." Ethan looked at Noah.

"I didn't either, but I do now." Noah leaned over the table. "Want to fill him in, Ken?"

Ken shook his head. "This isn't making sense. I told you guys everything, I promise boss."

"Then why did I find this among Lilith's possessions?" Noah held up the form he filled out moments before and kept it close. "It's a sexual harassment form she filled out against you the other day, Ken."

He shook his head and looked at Ethan. "I didn't do anything to her."

"Ken Ennis leaned over and grabbed my backside." Noah read his own words and handed the paper to January. "Right there, in *her* own words. Take a look, January."

January held the form close and nodded. "Wow, Ken, I always knew you were disgusting."

"My hand barely grazed her!" Ken shouted. "I apologized!"

Noah smiled, shoved his hands in his pockets, and shrugged at Ethan.

He bought it.

Pete rested his hand on Ken's shoulder and pulled him back against his seat.

"Why didn't you tell me?" Ethan stared down at Ken.

"I didn't think she'd make a big deal out of it. It was an accident."

"You want to be straight with me, Ken? I'll ask you one last time."

Ken's face turned several shades of red and Noah enjoyed every color to the fullest.

"How about I help you?" Noah rested his hand on the back of his seat. "Ken was more a partner with Arnold than he ever said because Ken got to pick the victims. You chose Lilith because you knew she was going to tell on you. You knew you'd lose your job after she filed a sexual harassment charge against you and you decided to have her killed instead."

Ken stared up at him but kept his mouth shut.

"How about Lisa?" Noah asked. "What could she have *possibly* done to you to deserve death?"

"Answer him." Ethan said.

"She cheated on me." Ken's hands shook and the metal cuffs tapped against the table. "I caught her in bed with some asshole."

Noah nodded. "And Georgia?"

"The nosy neighbor told my wife I was having an affair." Ken spat. "She's the reason we got divorced!"

"So you *killed her*?" January seethed.

"I felt bad about Lisa, she was the first— " Ken looked up at Ethan with watery eyes, "after he did it, I felt sick, but that bitch Georgia deserved it. She ruined my marriage, Lisa embarrassed me, and Lilith was about to have me fired! I got a chance to take control and I did."

"How?" Ethan let the question go like a puff of air.

"Arnold told me if I helped him, he'd let me choose. He told me he'd kill whoever I wanted. It didn't matter to him, as long as he got Avery."

"You what?" January glared at him. "Just took him up on the offer? You sick sonofabitch!"

Ken turned to her and smiled. "You were next. Maybe you still are."

January froze and looked from Ethan to Noah.

Noah nodded down at the paper.

Show him.

She slid it in front of Ken and stood.

"Goodbye, Ken."

She strode out of the room while Ken looked down at the fake report.

"You fucking bastard!" Ken screamed at Noah. "You faked it!"

"Pete." Noah nodded to him, and he pulled Ken up from his chair.

"Ethan, you promised me! I signed the agreement!"

"I told you what would happen if I found out you were lying."

They watched as Pete led him from the room, and for the first time, Noah felt traction.

⸺

As soon as Charla sent the text, she regretted it.

Avery woke her when she got back from the bathroom, and she couldn't go back to sleep.

She wondered what place January would decide to send her, and what she would do when she got there.

Get a place to live, a job, and that's where the vision ended and the memories began. She tried to look further back than the past month, but when she tried to relive a memory, she questioned each one. Aunt Maggie taking her shopping turned into her mother Maggie, and how happy she must have been to spend time with her daughter. How happy she must have been to know her daughter considered her to be her best friend. How sad she had to be when she dropped her daughter home to the ones she thought were her parents, and what Maggie returned home to.

The abuse.

She shook the thought from her mind, and stared at the ceiling. Three weeks since she had seen her dad's smiling face, eaten her mom's home cooked meals, or laughed with Maggie. These people, her parents, her aunt and uncle. They watched out for her. They protected her.

They gave me the best life they could.

They gave their lives for me.

She tried to imagine what had happened in the kitchen in those last few minutes of their lives. If they had seen it coming, or if he had attacked without words, without feeling.

In their last moments...

Her chest heaved, and she ached from a place inside she didn't know existed.

The feeling overwhelmed her, more than the days after their murders that she spent around toilets, more than the words Patty spoke that ripped through her.

Gone.

This was emptiness, she thought, and started rocking back and forth.

She reached out, and squeezed her pillow in her hand. She reached further and grabbed at the air.

Nothing and no one.

No one could ease the pain, or take away any part of what had happened, but she reached out anyway.

She reached across the couch to the floor and found her phone.

Mom. Dad. Maggie. Why did you leave me all alone?

She scrolled to Maggie's name, and beside it—Arnie.

She tapped the screen and typed.

She typed the words as they poured from the unknown place inside.

The needy place that scared her.

She typed until her index finger tapped the send button and then she let go.

The cell phone crashed against the floor and Avery turned over in her sleep.

The familiar pang of regret crept through her as she reached down for the phone. The feeling was sick and achy, but it was also recognizable.

The screen glowed over her face as she whispered her words out loud.

"I have questions and I need answers. Can we go back home?"

Chapter 52

Noah strode through the door with a tray of coffees in his hand and a smile on his face.

Ken was locked up for good and Tansy was analyzing his communications with Arnold. Noah had a chance to shave and have a proper shower before getting back to the department, and he had stopped at Joe's Cuppa on the way. He thought about his discussion with January about Avery, and wondered what she would have said if he told her everything.

How he was curious about Avery from the start, in a more personal way than he could even admit to himself at the time. How Avery let him in— how she showed him her vulnerable truth and how he accepted her. How it broke his heart to see her in pain, and how he noticed how she looked at him too. That it was his favorite part of the day, like a drug he couldn't wait to get more of.

And as he entered the station, he thought of telling January that the reason nothing had happened yet was about respect. His respect for his job and his respect for Avery.

As the lines blurred between truth and lies, and the case became more complicated, his feelings for Avery strengthened, and the will to protect her became too strong to shrug to the side for the sake of his job.

When he got to their office, he tapped on the door.

Avery opened it and her eyes lit up when she saw him.

"How'd you sleep?" He asked.

She shrugged. "They're still sleeping. I'll take those in."

He held onto the tray, and looked down at her. "Do you want to go for a walk? Get some air?"

She nodded and took the tray from him. She brought it into the room, and removed two coffees.

"Ahem," Sadie cleared her throat, "Avery, where are you going?"

"Noah's here. He brought coffee."

"Nice."

"Yeah, we're going for a walk, okay?"

Sadie grinned and nodded, before turning back over.

Noah noticed Charla curled up on the couch with her back to them.

Avery handed Noah a cup and they walked down the back hall in silence.

He opened the back door for her, and they started out toward the pond behind the building.

The sky was gray with white puffy clouds reflected in the water.

"How are you holding up?" Noah asked.

"I don't know."

"I know it's been hard staying here, but it's the best way to protect you right now."

"Actually, I wanted to talk to you about that." They stopped in front of a bike rack, and Avery leaned against it.

"Okay."

"Josh and I talked this morning. He thinks I should relocate, and he wants to do it with me. And Sadie."

"To where?" Noah's chest tightened.

"Not sure. I told him I'd think about it. I mean, I think it might be a good idea, but I wanted to run it by you first. I mean, I can go if I want, can't I?"

Why is it suddenly so hard to breathe, Noah wondered, and sipped his coffee.

"I said it before, and I meant it. You're safer here than you would be anywhere else."

"I can't live at the police station."

"I meant with me." Noah took a step toward her and she stared up at him. "I can keep you safe."

Avery rested her hand on her chest, "I don't know what's going on between us, but you've been cold with me. Distant since we saw each other again."

"I've been trying to catch a killer, Avery."

"And I've been trying to stay alive." She looked at the ground.

"There have been so many times when I wanted to be there for you, be with you," he lifted her chin with his fingers, "and I'm telling you now that I will be. That you can trust me."

"Nothing has changed, Noah. Why are you telling me this now? Why not before at the hospital? Why not when you first felt this way?"

"I've always felt this way and I've always tried to protect you."

"But what's changed, Noah?"

"Nothing. Everything. I've seen you go through so much, and I want to be there for you." He took another step closer, and their legs brushed against each other. "I want to go through this with you."

"You've got a job to do." Avery looked past him. "It can't work right now."

"It's dangerous, and you're life is at stake, Avery. Protecting you as an inspector isn't enough for me anymore. I want you to be in good hands. In the best hands. I can be that for you. I'm putting myself out there as an inspector and as a man. You believe in me, you trust me, and you feel it too, don't you? The energy between us. The thing that connects us?"

He leaned in and brushed his cheek against hers as she nodded.

She smelled like peaches.

"I feel it." she whispered. "I've waited for you to say these words, but I'm scared."

"I want you to stay," His gruff voice turned soft, "Avery, will you stay with me?"

Avery rested her hand on his arm, and as their cheeks brushed once more, she squeezed it.

Noah's lips found hers before his heart could beat again, and he didn't care who saw them.

His mind was lost in Avery.

⸺

When he whispered in her ear, before he even asked the question, she knew the answer.

She steadied herself against him, and before she could speak, his lips crushed into hers.

They were cool and his tongue was warm. Her heart beat faster and she pressed her hand against his chest.

When he pulled back, she looked around the pond to see if anyone saw them.

She looked back across the lot and realized his eyes hadn't left hers.

"I don't want to get you in trouble." She whispered and he stared at her lips.

"I was in trouble the day I met you." An edge came back to his voice. "I don't feel like there was ever an option to walk away from this. Not really."

"Noah."

"It's not a bad thing. It's the only good thing to come out of this. No apologies about the past or going forward, okay?"

Avery looked up at him, pushed off of the bike rack, and tucked her hair behind her ear.

"What now?"

"Now you know that I've felt this way for a while. Now, you tell Josh you're going to stay, and tell him he needs to come in. Tell him it's an order."

Avery pulled her phone out of her pocket and typed.

Call me when you get this.

"He's important to me."

"I know."

She nodded and took a deep breath.

"Let's go back in, alright?"

The cool breeze swept past them and Noah looked up at the dark sky.

"I think it's going to pour." He said, and they heard a beep from her phone.

"One sec, it's probably Josh."

Avery stopped walking and read.

If you want to see Josh again, you'll have to see me first.

"Noah," she pushed the phone at him and he took it, "Noah, he's got him. He's got Josh."

"We don't know that." Noah read the text to himself."We have to stay calm. Come on."

Rain poured down on them as they ran hand in hand back to the building.

Chapter 53

"I CAN'T GET A TRACE on it." Tansy stared at the cell phone beside her on the table. "Maybe he took the battery out?"

"He's going to try to get Avery alone with him. He'll set up a meeting time and place with his conditions." Ethan said. "Joshua Hopkins is as good as dead if we don't get to him before that meet time."

"We have to think through all possibilities," Noah looked to Pete, "to think about when and where he'd pick."

"If he took Josh this morning, and he expects Avery to meet him somewhere soon, he won't be more than a few hours away." Ethan looked at the map.

January hurried into the room. "Veronica, the woman who manages the shelter Josh works at, said he was there this morning for his shift, but that he went outside to his car and never came back. She didn't call it in before because Josh's car was gone. She figured he had an emergency. Arnold has his car."

She handed a folder to Tansy, and stood behind her. "That's the plate. Run it, check it against security video in this area, get it in the system."

January went to the map and tapped the spot where the shelter was located.

Ethan wrote the plate number on the board. "Pete, we need a B.O.L.O for this car and that plate in the system. Now."

Pete jogged to the door.

"Get back here afterward." Noah called.

"Do not give Avery and Sadie their phones back." Ethan told Tansy.

"They both want to talk to you Ethan. I guess you can tell them whatever you want to yourself." January sat down across from Noah.

"I want them protected. No meetings right now." Ethan looked across the table to Tansy. "How close are you to setting up secure location transportation for Charla?"

"I can have it done tonight, sir."

They all turned to her, and stared.

"Tonight?" Ethan asked.

"Right. Eleven o'clock, she'll be ready to go. January needs to tell her the location and Charla will buy a ticket at the airport. Money from her parents estate will be transferred to her bank account as soon as possible, and until then, I have sent funds."

Ethan turned to January. "Then that's what we do. That's how we protect her and stop her from being used as a pawn. As a distraction."

"Good." January said. "I'll tell her eleven. Ethan, I know you don't want to talk to them, but we can't keep them in the dark." January pressed her lips together.

"What? Fine, get them in." January slipped out and Ethan lowered his voice. "I'm going to tell them we have a trace on Josh's car and that we are working on locating it. That the text Arnold sent was just a part of his game. I want the illusion of control. You let me do the talking, alright?"

Noah rested his elbows on the table. "I have to tell you something before they come in, though."

"Go ahead."

"Avery and I, there's something going on between us."

Noah caught Tansy staring at them over her laptop, and when she realized she shouldn't be listening in, she tapped on the keys again.

"Oh, God. What are you saying Noah? You slept with her?"

"No, no. We just both feel a certain way about each other, and I want you to know because I don't keep anything from you that relates to my job."

"Great." Ethan stood up and crossed his arms as he studied the board with his back to Noah. "I've gotten more screwed over by my subordinates in the last month than I ever have in my entire career. I put together a team I trusted and relied on. I question my own judgment now that Arnold has used my people against me."

"If you want me off this case, I understand, but I think it motivates me, Ethan. I think it always has. It's the reason I brought Avery's case to your attention in the first place. I believed there was something more to this. I believed in her."

Ethan didn't make a sound.

"Like I said, if you want me off the case, I get it, but I'll still be protecting her. I'll still be involved somehow. I'm still the right person for this Ethan, and you know it. Ken was feeding Arnold information— that was the main reason we couldn't get a hold of him— but now he has no intel. He's injured and on his own. This is our time."

"I don't want you off the case. If I've been short with you since the hospital, I'm sorry, but I had to get Palfry outta here. The only way I could do that was to show him who's in control. You'll learn, and maybe you'll even learn *from me*, but I want you to keep your head in the game. I put my job on the line here to get Palfry off our backs. It's just us now. Can you tell me that you're focused?"

"I am. I know I can help."

"I need a team I can count on."

"You can count on me."

"Good." Ethan turned around, unbuttoned the top of his dress shirt, and sat down with ease. "I need a coffee."

Chapter 54

"I'M SORRY THIS HAS HAPPENED to your friend Avery," Ethan said as they gathered around the table, " and Sadie. You have my word we are all doing what we can to find Josh and Arnold."

Sadie tucked her foot under her, and pulled her chair into the table. "What are you doing about it?"

"We are tracking his vehicle at the moment. Tansy, our technical analyst is following the trail through multiple surveillance videos."

Tansy looked up from behind the computer and nodded to them.

"Has he messaged again?" Avery asked, and looked at her phone beside Tansy.

"No," Ascott said, "but we expect him to reach out, through your phone, or Sadie's. That's why we need to keep them here. We need to get ahead of him. Avery and Sadie, do you know of any place that has significance to you and Josh?"

"Where he saved me." Avery said, and bit her bottom lip to fight the tears.

"Right," Ethan sat down, "we've got surveillance on both Birch Falls and Crown River Parks. If he goes there, we'll see him before he even goes in. Anything else you can think of?"

Sadie shook her head. "Just his place."

"Right, we have that under surveillance as well. Charla, I called you in here because January and Tansy were able to work together to secure your transport. We'll have an officer escort you to the airport. January will tell you about your location after our meeting. Avery and Sadie, a secure location is something we can offer you as well."

"Can you?" Sadie asked.

"Arnold found out about the safe house because he was told by a member of the team. January is the only one who will have access to Charla's location. One person would do the same for you."

"How can you guarantee no one will tell?" Sadie crossed her arms and looked up at Ethan.

"January has your best interests at heart, and so would the other person designated to your relocation." Ethan turned back to Charla. "Tansy has set up your ride to the airport, so you have to be ready at eleven tonight."

"I don't want to go anywhere," Avery fought the urge to look at Noah, "I don't want to run away, and look over my shoulder. I want him caught. I want to bring Josh back."

"I understand, and you are under no obligation to leave. I have assigned January and Noah to your security. They will be with you both at all times."

"I want to know about Josh. When you know where he is, will you tell us?" Avery asked.

"When he is safe, we will let you know." Ethan nodded.

"No," Sadie said, "we want to know where he is as soon as you do. That he's safe as soon as you do."

"Sir?" Tansy spoke up. "You need to see this."

Ethan got up and walked around the table. "January, please escort the girls out now."

"We want to know— "

"Now." Ethan looked up at January as she ushered Charla out of the room.

"We can't waste time." Noah said, and Avery and Sadie followed.

When they got to their room, Avery and Sadie sat on the couch, and January and Charla sat at the table. They spoke quietly over an open file folder, and Avery felt the tension in the room.

"Sadie, I have to tell you something."

Sadie's eyes opened wide. "What?"

"This morning, I was talking to Josh. He suggested the three of us move away somewhere."

"He did?"

"Yeah, he wanted me to talk to you about it. That was just a bit before Arnold texted me."

Sadie pressed her hand to her mouth and shook her head.

"I know. I told him I'd talk to you and think about it." Avery rubbed Sadie's back. "That was the last thing I said to him."

"I don't even know what to do." Sadie cried.

"I know."

"Josh has been here for me too, while everything was going on with you. When you were in the hospital, or gone away, he was here for me." Sadie shook her head and tears flew from her cheeks. "I would. I'd move away, just the three of us. I'll do it Avery. I'll do it if he'll just come home."

Sadie broke down and Avery hugged her as she sobbed.

"He's strong, he can get through this."

Avery pulled Sadie closer and they wept together.

Chapter 55

"This is it. Pete brought this in earlier." Tansy clicked play, and they watched an empty road outside a gas station. "This was the last place caught on video."

Josh's sedan drove down the road, and Noah immediately recognized Arnold in the driver's seat. No other passengers were seen.

"Think he has him in the trunk?" Noah asked.

"If he still has him." Ethan watched the car drive out of frame. "Think he knew about the camera?"

"I don't know. He didn't go into the gas station parking lot. He just drove by. Probably not." Noah said.

"When was this?" Ethan asked.

"Eleven forty-five this morning." Tansy said.

"He's headed east." Noah stood up and went to the map. "What's over here?"

"The new subdivision being built." Ethan pointed to the place they set up. "You think Ken told him about it, so he went there?"

"Maybe. It's pretty empty at night." Noah said.

"Let's send some surveillance over there now." Ethan said. "What else is out east?"

The phone beside Tansy vibrated on the table.

She looked up at them, and Ethan grabbed it.

"Text." He leaned in for Noah to see as he pressed the button.

Cotter. Here's your chance. If Avery wants to see her hero again, and have the chance to save HIS life, bring her to Tipper's Point at nine o'clock tonight. I'll be there waiting, but if I see another pig, he's dead.

"Shit," Ethan muttered.

"At the hospital, he told me he didn't pick me because I'm inexperienced. He did it because he knew I'd set up the meeting with Charla for him. That I was too eager to catch who he was working with. That he knew I'd choose finding out who it was over the welfare of Charla."

"He's trying to play you." Ethan rubbed his forehead. "He thinks he can manipulate you into thinking it's about you and him. A cat and mouse game, but it's not."

"No, it's not. It's about the women he is killing. It's about stopping him from doing it again." Noah said.

"You're going to take Avery there, and we'll have back up surround the area after you go in. He won't be able to get out." Ethan looked at Noah. "We have to catch him."

"I can't put Avery in that situation. Take her back there? No. I'll go. She doesn't have to. Arnold said he'll be there anyway. I thought we agreed we weren't going to jeopardize her saftey?"

"Do you want to explain to Avery that if she's not there, he'll undoubtedly kill Josh? He's keeping him alive as leverage, Noah."

Noah shook his head, but Ethan continued. "We have a chance to catch him. To trap him. We can still save Josh, but Arnold has to know that you and Avery are there. He might think you'll bring her, and maybe he thinks you won't in an effort to prove him wrong about how much you care. If she's not there, Josh is dead for sure."

"No."

"Listen, I asked you if you could put your personal business to the side with Avery. We won't make her go, but what if she wants to?"

"If we ask Avery, she'll say yes." Noah said.

"How do you know?"

"The way she talks about him. He didn't just pull her out of the water ten years ago. He and Sadie pulled her out of a depression. She feels like she owes her life to him."

"If she wants to do it, I think we should."

"It can't be up to her. We can't put her in that position. What about a decoy?"

"Do you remember what I told you about Palfry? We have to catch him. Period." Ethan shook his head and sat down in his chair. "Noah, you prove to me that you can do what's right for this case, or you're off it."

Noah looked down at Ethan, but he wouldn't look up at him. He stared straight ahead.

He was serious.

"I don't want her getting hurt. If it was Sadie or Charla, I'd feel the same. This is his prime target, Ethan."

"But if the cuts on his victims are any indication, the countdown to ten isn't finished yet. If that's the case, he won't hurt her."

"Why does he want her there then? To watch Josh die?"

"It comes down to this. Do you think you can protect her?"

"Yes. I promised her I would."

"Then I've got my answer." Ethan stood from the chair, and walked to the door. "I'm getting Pete. You get the girls."

Chapter 56

Hold on, Josh. Please. Just hold on a little while longer.

Avery repeated the words in her head as she listened to what Ethan proposed. He explained the plan and the risks involved.

"Finally, I need you to understand that this is completely your decision. One way or the other, we support you, and if you don't go, we can send a look alike that might be able to work from a distance. It's up to you, and I won't lie, there is pressure to make the decision now."

"I'll do it."

"Avery, wait," Sadie grabbed her arm, and Avery turned to her, "this is a trap. It has to be. What do you think is going to happen? You go, and Josh runs into your arms, and the good guys catch the bad guy?"

"It won't be that simple." Ethan said. "Avery would be a distraction. She would make him think he's won his game. That we are complying with his demands. He won't be able to hurt her or escape. We'll have the place surrounded."

Sadie shook her head and choked out the words. "Josh might already be dead. Arnold might not even be there."

"I know," Avery said and grabbed her hand, "but if Josh is alive, and if Arnold is there, I can't let him get away again. I can't let him kill Josh because I'm not there. That will be on me."

"No," Charla stepped into Room C, "no. That will be on Arnold's head like the rest of this is."

Charla hung onto the door knob. "Josh wouldn't want you to go. Just remember that when you make your decision."

She slipped back out the door and Ethan sighed.

"We'll have you in a Kevlar vest, and Noah will be with you the whole time." Ethan said. "Back up units will surround Tipper's Point, and he'll be trapped in there. As soon as Noah gives us a confirmation on Arnold, we'll extract you, and the team will move in."

Avery nodded, and looked at Noah. "What do you think?"

"I'll be honest. I think he's playing a game, and we need to be a step ahead. I think we need to go, and make him think we're playing into his hand." Noah turned to Ethan. "If he's not there, where else would he be?"

"Tansy's working on it. I've already got eyes on incoming vehicles to and from the Tipper's Point area." Ethan said. "If we can get him to call us, Tansy can track him, but it has to be when you're both at Tipper's Point. It has to be then, when he thinks he's got us. Tansy will confirm his location."

"I need some air." Avery said, and Ethan nodded to Noah. "Okay fine, I won't go outside, but I want to talk to Sadie alone."

Noah nodded and sat back down.

"Can we go ahead with our plans then?" Ethan asked.

"I'll be back in a few minutes." Avery said, and Sadie followed her out the door.

On the way back Sadie went to the washroom, and when Avery entered their room, Charla and January looked up at her.

"What happened?" January asked, and Avery wondered if Charla told her she'd been eaves dropping moments before.

"Arnold texted my phone from Josh's again. He wants to meet me and Noah at Tipper's Point, or else he's going to kill Josh."

January stood from her seat. "You know you don't have to go, right?"

Avery nodded. "I just need to talk to Sadie before I make my decision."

"You're brave, Avery." Charla sat back in her seat and licked her lips. "When I saw you at Joe's Cuppa that day for the first time since high school, I didn't think you'd changed. Back at the safe house, you were different somehow, but I put it down to what we've been going through. January told me what happened in the woods with Fiona, how you tried to carry her, how you confused Arnold with the tracking devices. It didn't sound like the Avery Hart I thought I knew."

Avery put her head down, and tucked her hair behind her ear. "You didn't know me back then."

"I know, but I knew you were afraid. I knew I'd done that to you. What you said in that room— that was brave."

Avery nodded. "Thanks, but I'm only doing what Josh did for me."

"I'm telling you this because I wish I could be brave like you and I'm telling you this so you know you don't have to prove anything to anyone. I meant what I said. He wouldn't want you to go."

Avery looked into Charla's eyes and wondered why she was telling her this.

January took a step toward her. "If you need someone to talk to…"

Avery shook her head. "I need to talk to Sadie."

She hurried down the hall to the bathrooms, opened the door, and called Sadie's name.

"I'm in here." Sadie emerged from the last stall. "I have confidence in Josh. Maybe he can get out himself."

"Tell me what to do."

"I can't." Sadie said. "If it were me…"

"If it were you, you'd go. You're just trying to protect me."

"Do you really think you can go back there? After everything that happened to you in those woods?"

"For Josh? I know I can."

Sadie stood up and hugged Avery. "Then I support you. I just don't want to lose you. Maybe you really will bring him back."

Avery heard the distant tone in her voice, and squeezed her back.

"I'll do everything I can."

⤴

When Charla heard about the text Avery received from Arnold, she pushed her own feelings aside, and worried for their friend and what might happen to him.

She pushed her real feelings deep down, but the fact that Arnold had texted Avery twice made it impossible to stifle how she felt.

Jealous.

She had been angry that Arnold never messaged her back, but she was equally thankful. She sent him the message in a moment of weakness and grief. She reached out to the one person who had the answers.

Somewhere deep inside of her, she knew a part of her wanted to know the answers, and that part would do anything for them.

The despair she felt that night had passed and she woke to see another morning, but she couldn't suppress it any longer.

"January, you said those papers were ready, right?"

"For you to be relocated? Yes." January turned back from the door where Avery had left, and grabbed her coffee mug. "Everything is in order. I don't even know where you're going yet Charla, but you'll be safe. You have all my contact information, as well as banking in your file. You'll take that with you and go from there, and if you ever need anything, you call me."

Charla nodded and watched January sip her coffee.

"I was wondering if I could leave earlier than eleven?"

"It's not a good time." January set her mug down. "We're prepared for this, and I want to be able to see you off, so I've got to focus on the meeting with Arnold first."

"I know, but we can say our goodbyes now. I don't think I can stick around for this. You saw Avery. You know how this goes."

"Charla."

"I can't do it January. You've been so good to me, and you've helped me more than anyone, and I just need you to help me with this one last thing."

January studied her, and Charla wished she could read her thoughts.

"I'll see if Tansy can get your ride moved up."

"Thank you. I know you're busy and I really appreciate it."

January nodded. "I'll miss you, but I'm going to be so happy, thinking of you somewhere, starting over."

Charla thought she saw her eyes glaze over.

"Thank you for everything you've done for me January. I won't forget it."

"I won't forget you either. I want to hear from you when you're comfortable." January squeezed her arm. "If it gets to be too much in here, you can use Inspector Cotter's office to be alone, okay? I'll find you and let you know when it's time to go."

Charla nodded and as January went to leave, she stood up, and hugged her.

When she left, Charla sat down at the table, and tapped her fingers on it.

Only a little while longer, and I'll be out.
I can wait a little while longer.

Chapter 57

"You know I wouldn't be doing this if I thought I was putting you in danger." Noah opened the door for Avery, and she stood beside him as the sun touched the horizon.

"I know. I agree, this is what's best. This is what we have to do." Avery slipped into the passenger's seat, and looked out the window, toward the sun.

Noah shut the door, and as he came around to his side, Avery wished there was a way to get there sooner.

"I'll be there with you the whole time. Back up is right behind us. I'll call Arnold, you don't have to speak to him."

"Noah," Avery looked at him, "I'm not scared about going back there."

"Avery, don't lie to me."

She shook her head and looked into the sunset again.

"All I'm thinking about is getting to see Josh again. I'm not stupid. I know he could be— " She swallowed hard. "I'm just trying to be positive. It's the only thing that got me here. Thinking that he's out there, waiting for someone to find him."

"I appreciate you doing this." Noah started the car, and put his arm behind her seat as he checked over his shoulder.

"Charla was right, Josh wouldn't want me going."

"I know that, but maybe he'd change his mind if he knew I'd be with you."

Avery tightened her grip on her phone. "That's the reason I'm not afraid."

They backed out of the lot, and Noah radioed to Ethan.

As they pulled onto the road, Avery knew there was no going back. Josh could be mad at her, and he would be, but she couldn't leave him behind.

"What are you thinking right now?" Noah asked.

"I spoke with Sadie before I left, and she told me she supported me. I also spoke to Charla. She told me I shouldn't go."

"She did?"

"Yeah, but that's not what I was thinking about. She also told me I'm brave." She felt a lump in her throat and she swallowed hard. "I'm not the same girl who was dragged into the woods with Fiona. It changed me. She changed me."

"I know." Noah said, and someone came in over the radio.

"Everything's in place."

"I'll talk to him." Avery said when the signal was clear.

"Arnold?"

"On the phone. Yeah. I want to tell him something."

Chapter 58

A FEELING OF DREAD washed over Noah, as they approached the broken sign and stopped just before the entrance to Tipper's Point.

"You ready?"

Avery nodded and they got out of the car.

They walked to the entrance, where the gate used to be, and stopped. Noah listened, but there was no sign of movement.

"In position." Noah said.

"Copy." He heard Ethan in his ear.

Avery looked down the road at the place she and Fiona had found their way out of the woods.

The air smelled like burnt leaves and she shivered in the cold.

"Make the call. Tansy is ready." Ethan said, and Noah touched Avery's arm.

She looked up at him, and when he nodded, she opened the phone.

"This feels wrong, dialing Josh, and knowing it'll be *him*."

Noah watched as she hit the call button, and put the phone to her ear. He tapped her arm, and she hit the speaker button.

The first ring echoed out into the night, then the next.

One after another.

Then a click.

"We're here." Avery said.

"I know."

It was Arnold's unmistakable voice. He sounded content.

"Where's Josh?"

"He's here." Arnold said.

"Let me talk to him."

"You'll see him soon."

Avery looked up at Noah, and he nodded.

"Where do you want us to go?"

"Cotter knows where I am. He knows where I cut those girls up. He'll know where to find me. Cotter?"

"What?"

"I was right about you." Silence filled the air, and before Noah could speak, Arnold laughed. "I knew you cared more about finding me than helping Avery."

"I came here because I wanted to." Avery said.

His laughter died off and he coughed. "You didn't want to—"

"I came here to look you in the eyes, because I can see your eyes Arnold. I can see them with the mask on or off. I came here to look you in the eyes and tell you I'm not afraid of you. Show you I'm not afraid of you. Why don't you show yourself?"

Noah could hear Arnold's heavy breathing.

"If you still have Josh, if he's still alive, I'm offering you a trade."

Noah looked at her and shook his head.

"Tansy got it." Ethan's voice in his ear. "He's at a farm in Cedar Ridge. Sending the location. Meet us there."

"I'm offering myself in his place." Avery continued.

"Cotter." Arnold's voice grumbled.

The heavy breathing sounded distant, and Avery held the phone up to Noah.

"We're on our way."

Arnold hung up and Noah grabbed the phone from her.

"Why did you say that?" Noah asked.

"I wanted him to stay on the line. I wanted him to know I'm not scared."

"He's not here." Noah grabbed Avery's hand. "He's in Cedar Ridge. At a farm."

They ran back to the car and he closed the door behind Avery.

We might be a step ahead after all.
We found you.

Chapter 59

Sadie paced the room, and looked out the door every few minutes. She wouldn't talk to Charla, and when she asked if Sadie would sit down with her, she ignored her.

Charla left the room without looking back, and turned down the hall toward Room C. The back exit was straight ahead and it was dark.

Time's running out, she thought as she approached the room.

He won't stop.

Charla knew it in her core, felt it in her bones.

The only way her father would stop killing was if he was killed.

"I have to get back." She heard January's voice. "Tansy, when you get those files for Charla ready, could you call me? I know you're busy now— "

"I'm sorry," she heard Tansy's sweet unmistakable voice, "I can't right now. I sent them the location, and I have to be ready."

"Right, I understand, but when they're back?"

"I'll try, but I can't promise."

Charla slunk back down the hall and turned right toward the back exit.

It won't be ready in time.

She turned left, and found her way to Noah's office. She shut the door behind her, and cleared her mind with the help of silence in the small room.

She sat down in front of the desk, and wondered where January would send her.

Another country like Australia? Another province, maybe British Columbia?

Wherever she went, someone else would know where she was.

And that someone could tell Arnold.

She couldn't imagine January disclosing the location.

Even if she was tortured?

Her cell phone vibrated in her pocket, and when she checked the text, an unknown number accompanied it.

She read it twice.

If you come alone, I'll tell you what you need to know.

Charla stood up and went for the door, but she stopped before it.

Come alone.

Her legs shook as she thought about confronting him alone.

Niece to uncle.

Father to daughter.

She tucked her phone into her pocket, opened the office door, and peeked outside.

An officer in a cubicle, but no sight of January.

She snuck back down the hallway, out the doors, and into the night air.

She took a deep breath and felt her pocket vibrate.

She stared at the message.

Come home, Charla.

That was it. That small, insignificant detail was a sign.

She walked briskly through the parking lot and checked over her shoulder as she crossed the street. No one was coming to look for her. No one knew she was gone. Yet.

When she got across the street and out of sight, she searched through her phone for a cab company.

Last chance, she thought, as she dialed the number.

"Crown River Taxi."

"I'm at the corner of Ambrose Road and Garnet Street."

"Okay, and where will you be going?"

"Home."

Chapter 60

TWO POLICE VEHICLES WERE parked near the old farm house, and as they drove up the long driveway, one drove on toward the barn across the field.

Noah rolled down his window, and Pete poked his head in.

"The house is clear. Ethan's driving on to the barn."

"Thanks Pete."

Noah drove across the field; to where Ethan parked, and tension filled the car.

With each bump, his stomach knotted.

"Noah? Do you think he's in there?"

"I don't know."

They watched as Ethan and another officer pulled the barn door open, and Noah saw Pete's car pull up behind them.

Ethan drew his gun and they went in.

Noah turned to Avery. "I need you to stay in here."

"No, I'm coming with you." She clicked her seat belt and it slid off her chest.

"I'll come right back out and tell you if there's anything. Anyone. I need you to stay here where it's safe."

Avery nodded and sat back. "Be careful."

Noah put his hand on the back of her neck and leaned into her.

"No matter what happens, you're going to be okay."

She stared back at him, but her eyes told him she didn't believe it.

He got out of the car and locked it behind him. He pointed to the car, and Pete raised his hand and nodded.

He jogged over to the barn and saw the bright flashlights searching the space.

"Ethan!" He hollered.

"Cotter," Ethan hollered back from the darkness, "don't let Avery in here."

He slowed down at the entrance to the barn, and when someone yelled clear, he dropped his hand from the place it hovered over his gun.

The searching flashlights all gathered in one place.

Josh's bloodied face and the rope around his neck. A flashlight scanned his body as he swayed from a rafter in the barn.

"Shit."

Noah stepped beside Ethan and lowered his flashlight to Josh's chest. Four slash marks across it.

"Hey," Pete called, "I found the cell. It was ringing in front of the barn here!"

He shone a light on the cell phone by the doorway, and the light flickered across the wall and back.

"Wait," Noah grabbed Pete's flashlight and shone it at the wall.

"Ethan," Pete said, "you're going to want to see this."

Ethan walked backwards toward them as Noah read the message.

Cotter, will you catch me before I catch her?

"Damn it," Ethan yelled, "That's all this is to him. A game."

He shone the light at Josh's body.

"A pawn."

"He's been dead a while. Real cold." Another officer called, and Ethan grabbed his radio.

"I need the M.E. here now. We've got a body. Joshua Hopkins."

"No."

A shriek came from behind them, and Noah turned back to see Avery's outline in the moonlight. "No, oh no."

The light reflected off her blonde hair as it blew in the wind, and her dark figure dropped to its knees as she screamed once more.

"Late night at the office?" The cabbie asked.

Charla ignored him and stared out the window.

As each streetlight passed them, she saw her own reflection instead of the dark streets.

She thought about the other night, when she texted Arnold from the dark place within, and she wondered what question she carried for him in the depths of her soul.

What do you want to know, Charla?

She wanted to know she was loved, and she had been at one point, but it was taken from her.

You want to know why.

Charla shook her head. Arnold wouldn't tell her that because he didn't even have the right answer. The true answer.

Her family died at the hands of a sick man who reached his breaking point.

This is yours.

It is.

You want to be brave.

I will. I'll look at him, not as a killer, or as an uncle, but as my father. I'll look him in the eyes.

And I'll know what to do.

You already know what you have to do.

"Should I take this street?" The cabbie lost his friendly tone.

"Yes. Can you drop me right there, at the corner, please."

"Sure. It's late though. I'd like to drop you closer. These—"

"Here is fine."

She slipped him her bank card, and he gave her the hand-held debit machine.

"Which one's yours? I'll watch from here and make sure you get in safe."

Charla passed him his machine and opened her door.

She slipped out and started down the middle of the road.

Toward the place she grew up.

Toward the place she fell in the street just weeks ago.

The place she screamed until she had no breath.

⟿

Avery screamed as she fell to her knees.

Josh's face was cut and bloody, and his chest had been slashed.

He was hanging.

Dead.

"No Josh." She called to him, but his name caught in her throat, and she bent over from the pain in her own chest.

She heard someone run toward her and she looked up at Noah's face, as he reached his hands down for her.

"Ooh," she batted his hands away, and clutched her chest.

"Avery." He grabbed her arms, and her whole body shook with her sobs.

He lifted her, and wrapped his arm around her to support her weight.

"Come on, I'm getting you out of here."

"He-he," Avery fought for breath, "he killed him."

"I'm so sorry Avery."

He ushered her back to the car, and opened the door for her.

She sat down on the seat, but the world was spinning, and she couldn't catch her breath.

"Josh," she whispered, and rocked back and fourth, "oh, God, he cut his chest! He hung him."

She looked up at Noah and his face was a blur.

"Avery," Noah rubbed her back, "Avery, he's not in pain anymore."

She felt Noah wrap his arms around her. Her body felt warm in his arms, and she cried harder into his chest.

"Why? Oh Josh, oh Josh, Josh."

Noah didn't speak as Avery sunk into his embrace, and her shaking began to ease.

"I want to get you back to the station. I'll get you back to Sadie, okay?"

Sadie.

Avery cried harder, wondering if her mouth would even open when the time came to tell her.

Selfishly hoping someone else would. That she'd already know. That she wouldn't have to speak the words.

Avery poked her head out of Noah's arms, and looked up at the sky.

"I'm sorry, Josh," she cried and bent over, holding her stomach, "ooh, I'm so sorry."

Chapter 61

Noah wrapped his coat around Avery, and she brought her legs up to her chest as she leaned against the car door.

She sat huddled like that on the drive back and Noah had a hard time focusing on the road.

Ethan insisted he take Avery back to the station and watch out for the girls with January, while they tried to gather any evidence they could find.

He hadn't said it, but Noah knew sending him back with Avery was a favor.

The message Arnold left for him swam in his thoughts as they crossed the border into Crown River.

Avery's phone chimed.

"You want to get that?" Noah asked. "It could be Sadie."

Avery stared blankly out the window.

Can you catch me before I catch her, Noah went over the words again.

You won't get close enough, Noah thought, and Avery's phone chimed again.

"Avery?"

She shook her head. "It's just Facebook. Can you pull over?"

Noah pulled to the side of the road, and as soon as she opened her door, she leaned over.

He rubbed her back, and her phone slid out of her hand onto the seat as she threw up.

The phone chimed again and Charla's name flashed on the screen.

"Avery, it's Charla."

"You can check it yourself." Avery hung out the side, and was sick again.

Noah opened the message.

I'm sorry for everything, Avery.
I'm going to make things right.
Stay brave.

Avery wiped her mouth on her sleeve, and sat back in the car.

"What did it say?"

"I've got to call January."

Avery closed her door, and Noah started back on the road again as his phone rang.

"January? Is Charla with you?"

"No, just Sadie. I think she's in your office. I told her she could go in there, but I can get her for you."

"Can you check?"

"Yeah, I'll go now."

"I'll wait."

He looked down at Avery, and she looked up at him with wide eyes.

"What's happening?" She mouthed.

"She's not here." January said. "What's going on?"

"She just messaged Avery that she was sorry, and going to make things right."

"Shit."

"We're on our way. Have Tansy track her phone if you can."

"I will."

"Call Ethan."

"Okay."

Noah hung up. "Can you try to call Charla?"

"She's missing?"

"Yeah, call or text. Anything. Just get her to respond."

"Okay."

Avery dialed the number, and the phone continued to ring until it reached voice mail.

"Nothing."

"Just keep trying."

Chapter 62

Charla walked toward her house and opened her phone.

10 Missed Calls

5 New Messages

The air was fresh and it surged through her lungs as she took deep breaths.

It's the only way, the voice inside her rumbled, *you know what you have to do.*

She pressed January's number and waited.

"Charla, where are you?"

Charla stopped in front of the place that used to be her home.

"Charla?"

She barely heard January's voice as she let the phone slip from her ear.

"I'm home."

All the lights were off inside, as they had been on the night she found her family.

The phone slipped from her hands and cracked against the cement. She forced herself to walk to her door.

The knob was loose and the familiar jiggling in her hand made her eyes well up as she turned it.

She opened the door, and saw a foot and leg covered in blood, but when she closed her eyes and opened them again, the image was gone.

The kitchen tile was clean and the house felt empty.

"Hello?"

She walked down the short hallway to the kitchen, where the light from outside illuminated the room.

She ran her fingers over the knives in the butcher block, pulled out the smallest one, and tucked it in her pocket.

Her hands trembled as she looked down the hallway to their rooms.

You have to ask him.

"Uncle Arnie?"

You have to tell him.

She heard a creak, and turned her head toward the garage.

Where she found the mask ten years before.

She put her hand on the knob and took a deep breath before she opened the door.

Noah pulled into the parking lot as January ran out the back door.

He rolled his window down. "January!"

"Charla," she yelled, as she ran to him, "she called me. She's at her house. I think he's there with her."

Avery opened the door, and stepped out of the car, as January pushed past her.

"I'm sorry, Avery." January dropped into the seat.

"I'm watching you go in!" Noah shouted through his window. "Get inside and stay there."

Avery nodded and turned back to the building.

"She told me she was home."

Noah watched Avery slip through the back doors, put the car in reverse, and sped out of the lot.

"I think he called for her. I think he asked her to come there. She called me, Noah. She's trying to stop him."

"Why would she go on her own?"

"I don't know. Maybe she knew it was the only way he'd be there. If she went alone." January's voice wavered. "She called me so we could catch him."

"He thinks we're still at the farm house."

"Then he won't be expecting us."

⌒

Charla reached her hand out, and felt for the familiar switch by the door.

When the lights flashed on, she recoiled, and blinked.

Arnold stood in the middle of the garage with the mask in his hands.

"I knew you'd come, Charla." He smiled up at her.

"How?"

"You forget that I know you. I know you better than anyone in the whole wide world now."

An image of her parents in the kitchen flashed before her eyes.

"I know you better." Charla stepped down onto the garage floor and crossed her arms.

"Did you tell them you were coming?"

Charla shook her head. "They know I'm gone though. They're probably on their way."

"Why aren't they here yet?"

Her heart skipped a beat, but she kept her face loose.

"Because we have to talk first. Isn't that why you asked me here? You know I have questions."

Arnold smiled. "I can't get over it. I *knew* you'd come alone."

"I have questions for you and then I have something to tell you."

Arnold shrugged. "I've only got time for one question."

He put the mask on, and Charla tried to control her hands from shaking by slipping them into her pockets.

"I know I don't matter to you, but that doesn't matter to me, because they are coming for you."

Arnold pulled a thick knife out from his pocket, and for a few moments, she forgot who he was.

In the moments that he walked toward her, she thought of him as an evil masked stranger.

"Ask your question, Charla."

"Did our family mean anything to you? Did you love them, or me?"

He shook his head. "You're just like the rest and I'm going to watch you squirm like your aunt. Like your mom and— "

"My dad." She finished for him. "You're my dad."

He stopped a few feet away from her.

She couldn't see his reaction, but she imagined him as her Uncle Arnie again, looking stunned.

"How?" The words slipped from the mask.

"I found out after you killed them. There are documents to prove it. I'm your daughter."

He shook his head.

"It's true! Maggie had me when you were broken up! She hid me from you, and so did my parents. My real parents. The ones who raised me. They kept me safe from you for all this time."

"No, not how *could* it be," he moved toward her again, "how did *you* find out?"

"What?"

"You think I didn't know?"

"How did you know?" She knew the door was close behind her and she prepared herself to open it.

"A man from the police department was helping me. He told me. I guess we found out about the same time. Seems one of us probably cared more than the other, though."

Charla turned to push back through the door, but he grabbed her, and yanked her close by her hair.

"My niece or my daughter. Makes no difference. You've never meant more to me than you do right now. Than you're about to." He grabbed her neck and pushed her up against the brick wall. "Are you scared, Charla?"

Tears flooded Charla's eyes, but she closed them and shook her head. She wrapped her hand around the handle of her knife.

"You should be."

She felt the knife stab into her chest and she gasped for breath.

"You're scared now." The mask nodded up and down and he jabbed the knife into her chest again.

She knew he was smiling.

"Now?" He laughed, and as he cut her again, she gasped for air, but gurgled instead.

They heard sirens in the distance, and as he turned in that direction, Charla stabbed the meaty side of his neck.

When he turned back to her, she imagined the smile draining off his face, as blood filled her throat and spurted from his.

She focused on his eyes and he stared into hers.

Charla tried to tell him she wasn't scared, but it came out as a gurgle.

BARE YOUR BONES

Her vision blurred as the light dimmed in front of her, and the world went gray.

Chapter 63

THE CLOCK'S STEADY TICK was audible again as their sobbing subsided, and Avery let go of Sadie to wipe her face with her hands.

The tile was cold beneath them, and Sadie blotted her eyes with tissue.

Avery studied her face as Sadie spoke. "It doesn't feel real."

"On the drive back, I felt the same way." Avery sat up with her back against the wall as tears slid down her hot cheeks.

Sadie looked up at the ceiling.

"I don't want to even think it," Avery wiped her tears as they continued to fall, "but I wish he just came in when we asked him to. Why couldn't he have just come in?"

"He didn't want to live like that. Like we are."

"I know," Avery's breath caught in her throat, "but now he's dead, and he wouldn't have been."

Sadie leaned against the wall and covered her mouth with her hands.

"I have to call Josh's parents." Avery sat up. "I have to call Veronica."

"I'll call them, okay?" Sadie rested her hand on Avery's arm.

"I want to." Avery sniffed and tried to imagine how the conversation would go.

"I know, but I don't think you should talk about it right now. You've been through enough, okay?"

Avery nodded.

"I need you to promise me something first." Sadie said. "I need you to promise me you won't blame yourself for this. You tried to get him to come in. We both did. You went to Tipper's Point to get him back. You did everything you could. Know this."

Avery stared at her, and closed her eyes to ease the burn.

She heard footsteps on the tile, and when she opened them, she saw Noah.

"What's happened?" Sadie pulled herself up from the floor.

"Is Charla alright?" Avery asked as Sadie reached down to help her up.

Noah's chest rose and fell.

"Charla was murdered."

Avery knew Sadie was looking at her, but she couldn't take her eyes off Noah.

"How?"

"I can elaborate later. I'm so sorry about Josh."

"I want to know what happened." Avery's voice trembled.

"Arnold messaged her while we were gone. He told her to meet him at her parents' house. She went."

"Why?" Sadie asked.

"Because she wanted to fix it." Avery sniffled. "She wanted to stop him. She thought she could."

"We found a knife at the scene. She injured him."

"How do you know?" Sadie asked. "Was Arnold still there?"

Noah shook his head.

"She warned everyone else." Avery whispered. "She warned Josh. Told him he wouldn't be able to over power him if he came for him. Why would she go?"

Noah stepped toward her and opened his arms. She walked into them and he pulled her in.

"I'm sorry we couldn't save them. I'm sorry we couldn't save Josh."

Avery wanted to cry, but her eyes burned instead, and she rested her face on his chest.

"Where's January?" Avery whispered.

Noah shook his head and she left his arms. "She's not taking this well. I'm going to stay with you both tonight. I just need to finish some things."

"I have to call Josh's family." Sadie said. "I need my phone back to call his family."

Avery wondered who would call Charla's, and for a split second, she forgot.

A whole family, wiped out.

His.

Noah brushed Avery's cheek with his thumb. "I'll be back."

As she watched him leave, she hoped Charla was back with her family.

At peace.

Chapter 64

ETHAN BARGED INTO THE room and slammed the door behind him. "I knocked on every door in the neighborhood. No one heard anything, no one saw anything, and no one knows where he went."

"I'm sorry, Ethan." January looked up from the table, but Ethan avoided eye contact.

Tansy looked like she had shrunk behind the computer and she focused on the screen.

"I made you responsible for the protection of those girls," he stood with his back to the board, "but I don't blame you for this. Charla snuck out of here. She left, and we didn't know, and we got there too late. Arnold distracted us. We can't let this happen again."

"You should blame me." January stood. "I was supposed to protect her. Watch out for her. She died because of me."

Noah watched as she hung her head and wiped her cheek.

"We could sit here for hours and argue this, place blame, but I'd rather catch him. Wouldn't you?" Ethan turned to them.

Pete opened the door and Ethan waved him in.

"I got the flash drive for the crime scene photos." He handed it to Tansy, and she plugged it into the computer.

"January?" Noah lowered his voice. "Do you want to leave for this?"

"No." January turned her chair toward the screen.

"Show us Josh first." Ethan said.

The first picture came up, a complete photo of Josh hanging from a rafter.

"Medical Examiner estimated his T.O.D. an hour after he was reported missing. The scene is determined to be the murder location, and therefore, it was determined he was killed upon arrival at the barn."

"His chest has four slashes." Noah said. "It's important to note that Arnold is branding him the fourth victim."

"M.E. Wasn't able to say whether the lacerations were the cause of death, or the hanging, but she is leaning toward the lacerations on his chest." Ethan stood by his chair. "Next photo please."

A picture of the writing in blood on the barn wall clicked into view.

"The message was for all of us, and singled out Noah and Avery. Can you catch me before I catch her. It's all a game to him, which he proves again later. Next picture."

Noah winced at the next photo of Charla slumped on the floor. January bit her lip.

"The markings are consistent with the other victims. She has five lacerations through her chest. Next picture."

A close up of the marks on her chest.

"These marks are the shortest we've seen, but also the deepest."

Noah found it easier to look at the photo without her face and studied the markings.

"Do you think it was because she injured him? Cut him with the knife we found, and he didn't have time?"

Ethan nodded. "Which tells us how important this body count is to him. Next."

The photo changed to the white garage door and another message written in blood.

Blood means nothing.

"The writing is sloppier here. He didn't have as much time to do it. He was at the barn in Cedar Ridge when the phone call was made to trace him, and he went to Charla's house immediately after, leaving the cell phone at the farm after texting her to meet him. Tansy?"

Tansy clicked a few keys and cleared her throat. "He wrote 'If you come alone, I'll tell you what you need to know', and then, 'Come home, Charla.'."

"From the message on the garage, we can assume that she told him she was his daughter. That's how she assumed she could get close enough to kill him. It's difficult to tell how much blood was his and how much was hers. They bled at the same time, on the same place on the floor, but we'll know how badly he's injured when we get the report back. He could still be using Josh's car."

"I'm on it." Pete started for the door.

"Hold on." Ethan called. "I want to tell you all that I've been told that if we can't get a handle on this, the RCMP is coming in. We're out of second chances. Every step we make has to be ahead of his."

"Yes sir." Pete nodded, and Ethan nodded back.

When he left the room, Tansy turned the screen off.

"This is the end of the line. We're off this case if we don't bring him in soon." Ethan sat down and rested his forehead on his hands.

As the words sunk in, Noah felt their weight. "What's the next step?"

Chapter 65

"I THINK THAT'S EVERYONE. I'll be right here, alright?" Sadie's mom looked at Avery through the rear-view mirror. "Don't be too long."

"We won't." Sadie opened the door and grabbed her bouquet of yellow flowers. "Let's go."

Avery held her single white rose and scanned the grave yard one last time.

They arrived after the procession of vehicles from the funeral home, and Avery insisted on waiting until everyone had left before paying their respects. Josh's parents hadn't tried to contact her, but from what Sadie heard from Josh's mom, she was sure Avery wouldn't be welcome.

Avery opened the door and stepped out into the sun. The breeze was cool, and it blew through the orange and green leaves that had begun to change color.

Sadie slipped her hand in Avery's, and they walked to the place the crowd had gathered— under a red maple tree.

"Did you see Asher?" Sadie whispered.

Avery shook her head.

As they passed the different headstones, Avery's legs began to shake.

"Do you see Noah?" Avery asked.

"No. I guess that's the point."

When they reached Josh's plot, they stepped under the shade of the maple, and read.

Joshua Hopkins, 1981-2014, A good man, son, and friend to all.

"You're a good friend too, Avery." Sadie leaned her head on her shoulder. "Don't forget that. Josh wouldn't want you to forget that."

"I shouldn't be here."

"Don't you say that. Josh wants you here. He'd give you a big hug right now."

The tears poured down Avery's face. "Oh, Sade."

"He would," Sadie hugged her, "he'd give us both a giant hug, and he'd tell us we're still family. He'd be happy we're staying together."

Avery nodded. "He'd be happy we have Jack too."

"He probably watches Jack and Louie play, you know." Sadie wiped a tear from her cheek and held her bouquet up. "We love you Josh."

Avery watched as she stepped in front of his plot and whispered words that were lost in the wind. She knelt down gracefully in her long dress, and set the flowers to the side of the stone. She stepped to the side and leaned against the tree trunk.

Avery stepped up to the stone, and looked down at his name.

"Josh, you don't know how sorry I am. You don't know how thankful I am for everything you've done for me. "

She knelt down and smelled the rose. "I love you Josh, and I'll always be grateful to have had you in my life."

The wind blew her hair in front of her face, and as she pushed it away, she saw a swirl of leaves in front of her.

"Is that you, Josh?" She sniffled and smiled. "I'll look after Jack for you, and I'll remember everything you taught me. I'll always miss you."

She set the rose against the stone beside his name. "And I'm not going to live my life scared. I'm going to live the life I have to the fullest for you, and for everyone he hurt. Everyone he killed. And Josh? You'll always be my hero."

Avery kissed her hand and tapped his name on the stone before she stood, and Sadie joined her.

"Do you think *he's* here?" Sadie asked.

Avery shook her head. "Doesn't matter. Come on."

She took Sadie's hand and they walked back to the car.

"All clear." Noah spoke into his radio.

"Still clear, here." January's smooth voice replied.

"On route." Noah walked along the graveyard path to his car.

"Copy that." Ethan said.

As Noah drove through the twists and turns, he caught up to Sadie's mom's car, and followed it out to the road.

Avery turned around and looked at him, and instead of the tear soaked face he expected, she smiled.

He smiled back.

When they arrived at Sadie's house, Noah parked on the road.

"You coming?" Avery called.

Her dress blew in the wind and the smell of burnt leaves filled the air as the sun's glow tinted everything it shone on a warm orange.

"There in a minute!" He met January at the front door.

"Nothing?" She asked, and Noah caught a glimpse of her red eyes before she slipped her sunglasses on.

"Nothing."

It had been just over a week since Josh and Charla were murdered, and no other bodies had been found. No missing person reports filed.

No messages left for Noah or Avery.

No sign of Arnold Henderson.

"What about you?" Noah asked as they started walking around to the backyard.

"Bob Pope is dead." He raised his brows, but January didn't look his way. "The doctors knew he wouldn't make it. The family got to say goodbye."

As they rounded the corner, they saw Sadie and her mom sitting side by side, and Avery sitting across from them. Noah and January sat and they formed a circle with their patio chairs. Louie chased Jack around them, and they rolled around down toward the garden.

"That's everybody, then?" Sadie's mom asked, and when Sadie nodded, she pressed play on her ipod.

Peaceful sounds of nature played, and when Noah looked to Sadie, she shrugged.

Rita reminded Noah of Sadie, from the way they dressed alike in a bohemian hippy style, to the way they spoke, light-heartedly, and their smiles.

"Thank you all for coming to the spiritual memorial ceremony for Charla." Rita smiled and nodded to them. "I invite anyone who would like to speak to say a few words, and then I will finish the ceremony."

Noah looked at Avery, and she smiled and reached her hand out for his. When he felt her soft hand in his own, he realized he felt better than he had in a long time.

"Charla was a sweet soul, lost too soon, and we are here to remember her, honor her, and send her into the spiritual world. Sadie, would you like to start?"

Sadie licked her lips and nodded. "Charla, I didn't know you well, but you were a smart and talented peer. You were beautiful, and I know so many girls in high school wished they had your looks. Your final struggles were heart breaking to all who have been touched by you, and I hope you are resting in peace now."

Rita nodded and pat her daughter on the back. "Who's next?"

They looked to January, and Noah had a hard time distinguishing what she was feeling behind her sun glasses. She shook her head.

"No pressure, dear. Just a few words?"

She nodded and tilted her head to the side. "I'll miss you."

Noah noticed Avery open her mouth, but January spoke again. "I'm sorry."

Her voice broke at the end, and Rita nodded. "Good."

January stood and started for the side of the house.

"Want company?" Sadie asked, but January shook her head and raised her hand without stopping.

"That's alright. " Rita nodded to Noah.

"Oh," he looked to Avery, "rest in peace Charla."

"Good, good." Rita smiled. "Avery?"

Avery squeezed Noah's hand and let go. "You thought I was brave. That's the first time anyone's told me that. I wanted to tell you that just by being in this world after everything that happened, that you were brave too. Your last message to me was not to forget it, and I promise you, I won't. May you finally rest in peace with your family. Your real family."

"That's nice, dear." Rita squeezed her hand. "Charla, may you finally rest in peace, and be reunited with your family."

"Thanks Rita." Avery squeezed her hand back.

"Always happy to help guide a spirit home."

"Thanks mom," Sadie stood, "do you need help with dinner?"

Noah took Avery's hand in his, and led her around to the side of the house.

"How are you?"

"Better than you'd think." Avery tucked her hair behind her ear. "You?"

"Still nothing." She wrapped her arms around him, and he stared down into her eyes. "You're beautiful, you know that?"

She craned her neck forward and he bent down and kissed her gently.

"Thank you for being here."

"I'll always be here for you, Avery."

"I know."

"Oh, hey," Sadie stopped as she rounded the corner, "you and January eating with us tonight?"

"Noah?" January called from the front of the house.

"Probably just eating in the car again." Noah said, and started for the front, "I'll be in later though."

When he got to the driveway, he saw January holding a young boy's hand.

"It was just a prank!" The boy yanked his arm away from her, and addressed Noah. "I'm sorry. It washes off. I'll wash it myself."

Noah turned around and saw the writing on the garage door.

5 down 4 more to go

"Who told you to do this?" Noah turned around, and the boy's freckled face turned red.

"Some guy. He gave me twenty bucks and the spray paint to write on the garage door when no one was watching. I waited a long time."

"How long?" January asked.

"Two whole days. You guys have always been here, though. How come you're always here watching?"

January crouched to the boy's height. "How old are you?"

"Nine."

"Nine's old enough to know better. If that man ever comes back, you go straight to your parents and tell them to call 9-1-1."

"Why? Is he bad?"

"Yes, and you shouldn't be talking to strangers, alright?"

"Whatever, lady." The kid walked backwards down the rest of the driveway, and when he got to the sidewalk, he ran to a house across the road and down the street.

"We need to wash this off." January said. "I'll go in and—"

"Noah," Avery called, and when she came around the corner, he froze, "are you sure—"

Avery stopped in front of the garage and studied it.

He could lie. He could form a lie that kept her safe, but he could also take the chance to be honest.

"Arnold paid a kid in the neighborhood to do it." The words were out without anymore thought, and he couldn't take them back.

Avery stepped back toward them. "What? How do you know? What does it mean?"

"The kid told us he was paid by an older man to do it." January said. "I'm sorry, Avery."

"What does it mean?"

Noah looked at January and cleared his throat. "Arnold has a count down. He marks his victims by cutting them and they're numbered."

Avery covered her stomach with her hands. "He's counting down to me."

"We think so, but we can't assume anything." January said.

"It's pretty clear." Avery pointed to the numbers. "How long have you known, Noah?"

"We theorized since the third, but—"

Avery shook her head.

"It's true," Noah said, "I couldn't tell you until we were certain, and after Josh…"

"Josh was just a number? Number four?" Avery raised her voice. "Charla was five?"

"Yes."

"When were you going to tell me? Seven? Nine? Or were you going to keep it from me?"

Noah saw the hurt in her eyes, and as she squinted into the sun, she reminded him more of the lost Avery he first met.

"I'm sorry. I don't know when I was going to tell you, or how, but I wouldn't have lied."

Avery shook her head. "You did. You lied by omission, Noah."

"Avery, this case is confidential, and we couldn't—" Avery held her hand up, and January stopped.

"I'd expect this from you, January. Not you." She glared at him once more before she ran inside.

Noah started after her, but January grabbed his arm.

"Let her be alone for a while. She's scared, and angry, and she's taking it out on you right now, but it's about that." January nodded to the garage. "It's about him."

Noah exhaled and pulled his arm away. "Alright."

"She'll see you were just trying to protect her."

"Yeah, speaking of that. What do we do? He's been around here."

"I'll call it in to Ethan, come on."

He followed her to the car, and before he got in, he looked up at the house.

*I'm going to protect you, Avery.
No matter the cost.*

Chapter 66

Noah didn't come back inside like he said he would, and Avery didn't know if she was glad or upset about it.

When she told Sadie about the garage, she told her mom, who rushed out to the front.

Avery saw the look of concern on Sadie's face, but before she could say one word about it, Sadie asked her if she was okay.

Avery told her she was fine, but it was a lie.

As she laid in bed beside her best friend, she knew she had done the very thing she was mad at Noah for, and she did it for the same reason he lied to her.

To protect Sadie, because she didn't want to tell her the truth, because it might hurt her. Scare her.

The truth was that she was more than fine.

She felt stronger than ever before.

Brave.

Arnold was playing a game, and she was the target, the prize, the grand finale.

He knew where she lived, who her friends were. He knew her past, about the most traumatizing event in her past, and he brought it to her future, but he wasn't the worst thing to happen to her.

Josh's death. That was the worst.

And Charla, and Fiona, and Blue, and all the others he killed.

Arnold created the game and he knew all the rules— if there were any.

He knew his opponent's weaknesses because he had infiltrated them. He threatened them, worked with them, fooled them.

He knew his goal and she was his end game.

What he didn't know was that Avery was going to win.

Coming in 2015

The Avery Hart Trilogy, Book Three

Don't miss these suspenseful reads by Emerald O'Brien

Expect Mystery, Suspect Everyone

The Duet
Darkness Follows
and
Shadows Remain

The Avery Hart Trilogy
Lies Come True (Book One)
Bare Your Bones (Book Two)
Every Last Mark (Book Three)

Acknowledgments

For aiding in the creation of this book, I'd like to thank my editor, Lindsay Miller, who has been there since the beginning. I'm grateful for her time and effort. To my formatter, Jade Eby, and my cover designer, Najla Qamber, for all professional visual aspects of the book that please my readers. I truly appreciate their hard work and talents.

Thank you to my Beta Readers: Jade Eby, for her writer's instincts, knowledge, and perspective. Steph Parks, for being my first true-blue reader, and providing me with a reader's passionate perspective. And my sister, Shyla O'Brien, whose opinions mean more to me than she knows.

I am truly thankful for the continued support, encouragement, and love from my family and friends.

To my husband, Aaron, who has helped to make my dreams a reality in so many ways. I am forever grateful to you for your love, support, and involvement in my passion. As always, I'm excited to see what's next with you by my side.

And finally, thank you to my true-blue readers, and my Street Team. You have spent your time with me and my stories, and I consider myself lucky to be in such good company.

You've all helped to make my dreams come true.

Sending love and light back to you.

About the Author

Emerald O'Brien is the author of new adult mystery Darkness Follows, and its sequel, Shadows Remain. Expect mystery, Suspect everyone.

Emerald is a Canadian writer, who grew up just east of Toronto, Ontario. She studied Television Broadcasting and Communications Media at Mohawk College in Hamilton, Ontario.

When she is not reading or writing, Emerald can be found with family and friends. Watching movies with her husband and their two beagles is one of her favourite ways to spend an evening at home.

Visit her website for more information:

www.emeraldobrien.com

Sign up for Emerald O'Brien's monthly newsletter and be the first to know the release date for Book Two of The Avery Hart Trilogy:
http://eepurl.com/YRhbX
You will also have access to exclusive updates and giveaways. Your email address will be kept private.

One of the best ways to support an author is by leaving a review. If you enjoyed this story, please consider leaving a review, long or short, where it was purchased.

Made in the USA
Charleston, SC
21 July 2015